To Madison,
Stephen Gilbert

Uncle Albert

STEPHEN GILBERT

ISBN-10: 1540631982

ISBN-13: 978-1540631985

DEDICATION

This book is dedicated to my daughter, Beckie. There's never been a day when the sight of her hasn't lightened my heart and filled me with pride.

CONTENTS

ACKNOWLEDGMENTS

I figure you're probably going to skip this section because it's not part of the story. Heck, I usually do. But you should read it, because I've included some interesting stuff.

First, I have to thank Mr. Johnson, the principal of my elementary school, and Mr. Ward, who taught sixth grade. They were good people who taught us a lot and made school a fun place to be.

My fourth grade teacher wasn't named Mrs. Mckenzie, but she really did tell us that we needed to work hard so that we'd be ready for fifth grade. And I remember sitting in homework detention more than once.

I guess that if you read the back cover, you know that I was a teacher and a school principal. One of my favorite memories is having lunch with the kids. Yes, first graders do like to talk about boogers. And principals get pretty busy, so it's hard to find time for exercise. I used to play basketball with the older kids. They ran me until I was about to fall over, but it gave me a good chance to get to know them and teach sportsmanship.

Except for the Uncle Albert's smoke lady, just about everything in this story is true. I can even remember the day I came in to the multipurpose room from supervising the little kids on the playground just in time to stop a food fight... and the angry calls from mothers whose kids came home with food on their clothes. Somehow, that was my fault. We had assemblies and pizza lunches and popsicles and plays, and lots of really smart, capable kids. I even tried to talk the teachers into a job switch adventure where kids, for just a day, would take over from the adults and run the school. Most of them didn't like that idea, but I thought it might be fun. Also, I knew that if we chose the right kids, the school might just run a little better.

Prologue

It all started with a simple question. One simple question. Not two, or three, or even twenty. Just one simple question.

"So what do you think we should do, Billy?" Mrs. Madigan phrased it like it wasn't a big deal at all, because really, doesn't everybody have an opinion most of the time? I do. Don't you? Well, I definitely had some ideas, so I answered. And that's why I'm in the fix I'm in today.

Hah, so I'll bet you're wondering what the problem is. It's a biggie, and you'll never guess what it is, never in a million gazillion years. Go ahead. I'll give you three guesses. In fact, you write them down somewhere, maybe inside the back cover of this book. Then when you see what happened to me, take a look. I'll bet you guessed wrong. And no cheating. Once you write down your guesses, you can't erase them.

Well, more on that in a little bit. First, a little background.

Chapter 1

The Letter

When I was nine years old, I found out that I had a great-great-uncle I'd never met before. In fact, I not only had never met him before, I'd never even heard of him before. His name was Albert, Albert Saloozian, and he was Grandma Ruth's father's big brother. Try and figure that out. I had to make a chart. Of course, since my grandmother died when I was just two, she didn't have a chance to tell me about Uncle Albert.

And you can't really blame me for not knowing about him since even my mother didn't know about her great Uncle Albert. Even my own mother! I guess Grandma Ruth forgot to tell her too. Or something.

Anyway, when I was nine years old, we got a letter from New York. I was in the kitchen when the mail came. Mom was making dinner, so she had me open the mail and read it to her, so she could tell which letters to keep and which to just toss out. That was one of my chores, but it was kind of interesting actually. Do you have any idea how many credit card applications your parents get in a week? It's scary. And some people fill out every one, even for their dogs and cats. I heard of one credit card that got sent to Rover P. Paws. Check it out. It's true! I wonder if he bought anything with it. Maybe tennis balls.

So we got this letter from New York. I opened it. "Dear Mattie," it said. That's my Mom's name, Mattie. "Uncle Albert asked me to write to you and tell you that he's traveling to California in December. He'd like to stay with you if that's all right."

That was the big news. "Who's Uncle Albert," Mom asked. She was stirring marinara sauce on the stove, so she couldn't look herself.

"I don't know."

"Well, who's it from?"

I looked at the return address. "It's from Beatrice Horflink and she lives on Fillmore Street in Watertown, New York. Who's that?"

"Oh. Beattie. She's my great aunt. I don't think you've ever met her." She stopped stirring for a moment and looked at me, but I don't think she really saw me. She was trying to remember something. "I don't think I've seen her since I was a girl." She went back to stirring. "Go on. What else does she have to say?"

"Uh," I looked back at the letter, "do you want me to read it all?"

"Sure."

"Okay." I started reading.

September 23

Dear Mattie,

Uncle Albert asked me to write to you and tell you that he's traveling to California in December. He'd like to stay with you if that's all right. He's going to be wandering all over the country and expects to be in your neighborhood on the 23rd. He'll be staying with you for three nights.

My mother scowled at me. "Really? At Christmas?" She went back to her stirring. I could tell she was upset, because she was stirring quite a bit faster now. "Go on. I suppose there's more."

We've been well here. Fall has definitely come in a big way. The leaves are just a glorious mass of color, but it's gotten chilly overnight. Last night the temperature dropped down to 29 degrees, our first frost.

My arthritis seems to be winning the war with my fingers. Knitting has gotten so much harder in the past couple of years, but I find it relaxes me to work on sweaters. I'll try to send some for your kids with Albert. I'm sure they need good warm sweaters.

Phillip is enjoying his retirement. He helps out at the Elk's Lodge on Tuesdays and plays golf on Thursdays. It keeps him busy.

Please write and tell me the kids' sizes for the sweaters. I've started a lovely one and will make sure that it fits with a little extra room for growth.

All for now,

Love, Beatrice

I looked up at my mother. "Really? I'm getting a sweater for Christmas?"

She didn't break stride with her stirring. "Hush. Aunt Beattie loves to knit. She's been knitting sweaters for all of her nieces and nephews since I can remember. I got a couple when I was a girl. I should think you'd appreciate a nice home made gift. Think of all of the hours she'll put into it."

Yeah, I thought, just what I needed. A sweater. Why didn't she save some time and go on down to the store and buy a real sweater, or maybe something useful like a soccer ball. "Okay," I said. "I guess." Then I re-read the first part. "So who's Uncle Albert?"

I had to read the letter again when Dad came home. They think it's good practice for reading in school. I'll bet you can guess his first question. Right. "Who's Uncle Albert?"

Over dinner, we tried to figure out where he'd sleep for three days at Christmas time. After all, it's not like we have a bunch of extra beds just floating around the house. We only have three bedrooms. There's mine, and I share that with Danny, my little brother, and then there's my sister's room, and Claire made it pretty clear that she didn't want any old man sleeping with her, so that left Mom and Dad's room, and that took care of that. No place for him to stay, unless he wanted to sleep on the couch. I figured we'd have to write back and say he couldn't come. Maybe he could keep the sweaters as a consolation prize.

Dad seemed to have a different plan. "Well, it's settled then. He can bunk with the boys."

Whoa, what? "Where?" I said. "Bunk bed, remember? Two beds, two boys. Where's he gonna sleep?"

"Simple. Danny can keep the top bunk. Albert will sleep in your bed, and we'll put down a camping mat for you on the floor. If we slide it under your desk, you'll hardly lose any floor space at all and it won't be in Albert's way." He looked down at his fork. "This is perfect spaghetti, dear. I love the marinara. It tastes like you put in a little more garlic."

And that was it. Done. Finished. Merry Christmas Billy, you get to sleep on the floor. Oh, and did we mention that you'll be under the desk so that you don't get in the way? Or that your payment for this is a new sweater? What happened?

Chapter 2

A Wasted Saturday

Things didn't get much better the next day. It was Saturday, my first day off school after a whole week. So what did I get to do? That's right. I had to write back to Aunt Beatrice. Why me, you might ask. Well, I guess writing practice is good for me too, and besides, Beattie is going to knit me a nice sweater.

Yeah. It didn't matter that I'd made plans to play softball with the guys. I had to call Paul and tell him I'd be late to the park because I had to write a letter. I could practically hear him laughing already.

Mom told me what to write. I tried to tell her that if she was just going to tell me, maybe she should write it. That comment cost me. Before writing the letter, I had to take out all the garbage. Should have just kept my mouth shut.

October 5

Dear Aunt Beattie,

It was so nice to hear from you. I'm happy to hear that Phillip has finally been able to retire. He's worked so hard and you both deserve to get out and enjoy life.

Billy is writing this letter for me. He's in fourth grade now, and we are very proud of him.

Danny just turned six and is an enthusiastic first grader.

Claire is in middle school, and very much a young lady who knows her own mind.

I'm certain the kids will love the sweaters. I remember the beautiful sweater you made me when I was a girl. I wore it all the time. I've written down their measurements on a separate piece of paper. Thank you for your thoughtfulness.

We're looking forward to Uncle Albert's visit. I don't recall meeting him before, but may have when I was a girl. The kids are very excited. Living all the way out here on the west coast, they so rarely get to see family from New York, so that it will be a special treat.

Write again soon with Uncle Albert's plans.

Love, Mattie

So that was it. Blah, blah, blah. I especially liked the part about me loving the idea of getting a new sweater for Christmas, or looking forward to meeting Uncle Albert, the guy who was going to take my bed. I tried to change some of that, but she reminded me that it was her letter. I was just the scribe, whatever that means. In the end, I figured that if I wanted to play softball at all, I should just write and keep my mouth shut.

She did offer to drive me to the park, so that helped. Of course, there was a mailbox on the way, so it wasn't really because I was in a hurry to get out and play ball.

When I got there, the guys were already in the third inning. Paul took me onto his team, and I got outfield. We lost, but since we were already behind 19-6 when I got there, I didn't feel too bad. After all, when I finally got up, I got a hit and scored a run.

Chapter 3

Uncle Albert

Over the next couple of months, I pretty much forgot about Uncle Albert. We heard back from Aunt Beatrice, but she just told us when he'd be coming on the train. The train? Really? Did people still travel on trains? I guess old people do.

So anyway, I got busy with school. I should tell you about Mrs. Mckenzie, my teacher. She hates kids. Now you might wonder how I can say that. I mean, aren't teachers supposed to love kids?

According to Mrs. Mckenzie, fourth grade was intermediate, not primary any more, and her job was to get us ready for fifth grade, which meant we had to be able to write reports, and do fractions, and all kinds of other stuff. And since she didn't have time during the day, we had to do a lot of it as homework. Did I mention that we had at least an hour every night? Bet you're not wondering now why I said she hates kids. Plus, she's strict. I got detention one day just because my pencil broke. It's true. I asked Alice, the girl who sits next to me if she had an extra one, and bam, detention. I tried to explain that my pencil was broken, and even showed Mrs. Mckenzie the broken lead. That earned double detention for arguing.

I told my mom, expecting her to talk with Mrs. Mckenzie, but she just asked, "Why didn't you have a spare pencil?" Some help.

I remember fourth grade now as the year when my hand was sore. I had to write all day in school, and then I had to do homework, and then I had to do my writing for my parents. Sometimes I wondered if my hand would permanently cramp so that I couldn't use it for anything else!

Well, after a long haul from August all the way to December, Christmas break finally came. I was more than ready.

The whole family went to the train station in downtown San Jose to meet Uncle Albert. He was coming on the Coast Starlight. I guess it runs all the way from Los Angeles up to Seattle. Sounds boring to me, but you never know with old people. I guess they like sitting for hours looking out the window. I'd rather fly.

We met him by the track, which was kind of cool. The engine was hissing and sputtering, like an old car, and we walked all the way down to the fifth passenger car. I was a little worried that since nobody had ever met him, we wouldn't know what he looked like, but Dad said it'd be easy. After all, how many old men would be getting off the train?

Yeah, right. Just about everybody on the train was old, except for a few kids who were obviously traveling with their grandparents. So we started to look for an old guy traveling alone.

Claire saw him first. "Could that be him?" she called.

Mom wasn't too sure, but we all walked over to ask.

There was this old guy, who'd just gotten off the train carrying a patched up suitcase, and looking around like he was lost and trying to find somebody.

When we got close, Mom called out, "Uncle Albert?"

He just looked up and smiled. "You must be Mattie." And then he saw the rest of us, "And your brood."

He was nothing like I expected. I mean, Claire was taller than he was, and she was just in seventh grade. He was wearing this jacket that looked like a green and yellow checkerboard over a stained white shirt, and when I got closer, I could see that his bow tie was a whole swirl of colors. Mom called it a paisley design later, so I looked it up, and sure enough, people used to wear clothes like that back when my grandparents were kids. And if that wasn't bad enough, he had bright yellow tennis shoes and a tweed hat with a green feather in it. Can you get the picture out of that?

And did I mention that Uncle Albert was old? I thought my Mom and Dad were getting up there, but Uncle Albert completely redefined old. He made Grandpa Jake look like a kid on his way to first grade. When he finally took off his hat, we could see that he didn't have hardly any hair on his head, just a sunburn and little white fringe that ran around and even stuck out of his ears. What really said old to me though, were his wrinkles. The man had wrinkles on his wrinkles. If you were an ant and you were trying to go from one side of his face to the other, you'd have quite a hike, if you didn't just get lost in one of the canyons.

Believe it or not, I heard Dad say later that he actually looked pretty good for 93.

Anyway, we all said hello, and Dad had me take his suitcase on the way out to the car. It wasn't very big, so that was okay with me. After all, maybe I'd find a chance to lose the sweaters.

Chapter 4

Sleeping With Uncle Albert

That night, Uncle Albert got to sleep in my bed, and I got the camping mat. It actually wasn't too bad. I'd slept on it before when we were camping, and it was pretty soft. The only thing I had to be careful of was waking up in the middle of the night and trying to sit up without getting out from under the desk. I did that once, and smacked my noggin on the bottom drawer. After that, I was more careful.

So, should I tell you what it was like trying to sleep with a 93 year-old man in the same room?

Not good! Got that? It was not good.

First, he snored. I woke up once from a dream where I was on the highway in an old diesel truck, but it wasn't a dream. Uncle Albert's snoring was so loud that even the windows were rattling. I tried putting my pillow over my ears, but that didn't do much good. Fortunately, I fell back to sleep.

Then there was old people smell. I'm not sure what they

fed him on that train, but what was coming off of his body was pretty vile. I was reminded of science class, where Mr. Wilson told us that hot air rises. Well, body temperature is 98.6 degrees, and the outside air in the room was about 70 degrees, and that meant that any gasses coming from Uncle Albert would be going straight up, and since I could smell it on the floor, I actually figured maybe I should go check on Danny to see if he was still breathing. He was, but it was pretty sickening in that top bunk, so I opened a window. In fact, our room was in the corner and I opened up both windows hoping for a breeze. I wouldn't have cared if it had been snowing outside, I opened those windows and then hung my head out breathing the clear cool air. It was heavenly. Then I went back to bed. I held my breath for as long as I could, but finally had to take a breath. You'd better believe that I was glad I got to sleep on the floor after that!

Chapter 5

Mumblety Peg

Actually, Uncle Albert was a pretty interesting guy once you got to know him. Take breakfast, for example.

There we were, sitting around the kitchen table, eating cereal and talking about what we were going to do. Claire wanted to go to the mall with her friends, which was natural, since she always wanted to go to the mall with her friends. Mom vetoed that right away, since it was Christmas Eve. Claire and Danny and I had to help with dinner for Christmas. I guess Mom had lots of vegetables to slice, and a turkey to thaw, and pies to bake. Boy would that be fun. I offered to thaw the turkey. I figured I'd take it out of the fridge, put it on the counter, and go outside. But no. I got vegetables. I sure couldn't wait to get my hands on that vegetable peeler. I could tell that Claire felt the same way by the way that she rolled her eyes.

Anyway, I got to peel about a hundred potatoes. It could have been worse. Claire got stuck slicing apples for the pie and vegetables for the stuffing. Since Danny's just a little guy, he got to decorate cookies. Now that would have been a good job, but I guess I was too old for that. Dad ended up having to entertain Uncle Albert.

When I got done, Mom let me go. Claire was helping Danny by then, and there wasn't room for me, so I skedaddled before she could change her mind.

When I got outside, there were Dad and Uncle Albert, laughing up a storm. You won't believe what they were doing.

"Come on over," Dad called. "Uncle Albert's been teaching me how to play Mumblety Peg."

"Huh? What's that?"

"It's a game I used to play when I was a boy," Uncle Albert said.

Great. I was going to get to learn how to play a game from back when they had to hide from dinosaurs. Then I looked down between them. They had a knife stuck in the ground. I recognized it as the one Dad carried in his pocket. He always said that every man needed to carry a folding pocketknife, and I got my first one when I was in second grade. I looked up at him, confused. "Mumblety Peg?" I asked.

Dad said, "You got your knife in your pocket?"

"Uh, it's in my room so I won't forget and take it to school."

"Well, go get it." When I just stared at him, he said, "Go on, get it."

So I ran back into the house and grabbed the knife. It was

buried in the back of my sock drawer so that Danny wouldn't find it, but I knew where it was. I was back outside in a jiffy, and ran over to the two men. This might actually be fun. Maybe it was a lesson in holding off dinosaurs with a knife. Did cave men even have knives? I held the knife out in front of me.

Uncle Albert looked at it and scowled. "That's hardly a knife," he said.

I looked down at the thin red Swiss Army knife in my hand. I was proud of that knife. It was all I had. I got it for my birthday when I was eight. It sure looked big then, but I had to admit that it looked pretty insignificant now.

"Here," he said. "Take mine." He handed his pocketknife over to me. Okay. Now that was a knife. It was long, about four or five inches, with a bone handle and two blades. He'd closed it before handing it to me, but after I had it, said, "Go ahead, open it up. Take out the big blade."

I reached my fingernail into the slot and pulled out the blade. It had a little dirt on it, but other than that, wow. It stuck out from me about as long as my index finger. You could do some serious whittling with something like that.

He looked over at my father and said, "Ok, Bill, show him what to do."

Bill's my Dad's first name. Guess how I got mine.

So Dad took his knife, and laid it in his hand so that the blade was sticking out next to his thumb, and then tossed it in the air. Sure enough it landed with the blade in the grass. Cool, huh?

Uncle Albert put out his hand. "My turn. Hand me the knife. That's right, handle towards me and blade back towards you. Somebody taught you well."

"My dad," I said.

He laid the knife on his palm, with the blade next to his thumb the same way Dad had, and moved his hand slowly up and down. Then he tossed it into the air so that the blade came down in the grass. He winked and looked at me. "Ready for your turn? Go get it."

I picked up the knife, and he helped me position it in my palm, and then said, "Ok, toss it."

I did and it landed, on it side, and bounced.

"No problem. It takes a while to get the knack. Let's try again."

After some practice, I was able to make the blade stick almost every time. That's when Uncle Albert told me about Mumblety Peg. He said he learned it in school from the older kids. Everybody had a pocketknife, and they played the game at recess.

Yeah. I'll bet you're wondering why he didn't get expelled for bringing a knife to school, but he said it was different back in the old days, when all the boys had a knife. Sounded like a pretty interesting school to me. Maybe they had to protect themselves from Saber Tooth Tigers or something.

Anyway, in Mumblety Peg, you push a stick into the ground. I didn't know why until the end, but more on that later. It was pretty disgusting. Then you take turns throwing a knife so that the point sticks in the ground.

They're lots of different ways to throw. The one I did first was the easiest, so that's where Uncle Albert started me. Next, I had to do it with my left hand. That was harder, but I got that one pretty well too. After that, we moved on to a throw where I had to hold the knife by the tip of the blade and kind of flip it so that it turned in a circle and stuck in the ground, and then two circles. And so on. Some of the moves were pretty complicated and only Uncle Albert could do them, like where he held the knife by the tip of the blade and flipped it over his head backwards. It must have spun around five or six times before the blade, you guessed it, stuck straight into the ground. After that one, he got to be the Mumblety Peg champion.

Remember the disgusting part? Uncle Albert said I was the grand looser so I had to go and get the stick, only I had to pull it out of the ground with my teeth. That's right. You didn't misread that, with my teeth. I was about to do it, when he laughed and said that since I was just learning, he wouldn't make me do that this time, but in real games, when he was in school, that's what the loser had to do. I thought he was going to make Dad do it, but he didn't. Actually, that might have made the game a whole lot more fun.

I figured this'd be a great game to teach Paul and the rest of the guys. I think a couple of them have pocketknives, and I'm sure you can play it even with the little knife I have. I'll have to practice though. I have a perfect record when it comes to never pulling sticks out of the ground with my teeth. I'd like to keep it that way.

Chapter 6

Presents

We're always up early on Christmas morning. Well, we kids are always up early. Mom and Dad usually roll out of bed sometime around seven. By then, we've had a chance to unwrap all of the presents, play with the stuff inside, and then wrap them up again. I don't think they've figured that out yet. We're really careful to act excited whenever we open something cool even though we already know what it's going to be.

This Christmas was just like all of the others, except for one thing. Uncle Albert was there, sitting in Dad's favorite chair, watching us go wild over our presents. I'm not sure I liked that. I mean, we've had family there before, like Grandma and Grandpa, and Aunt Kathy and Uncle John, but we knew them, and nobody sat in Dad's chair.

I mean, it was pretty cool learning how to play Mumblety Peg and all, but Uncle Albert's still basically a smelly old man and I have to sleep on the floor.

Once we finished opening all of our presents, Mom gave

him one. He was really surprised. "You didn't have to do that. Letting me visit and meet your wonderful family was gift enough. Thank you!" He fumbled with the wrapping, and finally got the box open. It was a new white shirt, exactly like the ones he'd been wearing every day. Well not exactly. It wasn't stained, so I guess it was better than the others. He held it up and thanked everyone again, and then said, "I brought some presents for you too."

He held a box out to me. "This is for Billy from Beatrice."

I tried to smile even though I knew what was inside. The sweater. Great. I opened the box. I looked inside. Dreading every moment, I slowly moved aside the tissue paper, and there it was. It perfectly matched Uncle Albert's green and yellow check jacket except for the stains. Wonderful. I'd be laughed out of school. Still, I knew what was expected. "Oh, a sweater," I said. "It's really nice."

"Hold it up so that we can all see it," Mom said.

Yeah. Make the humiliation complete. I held up the sweater in front of me. Claire was trying so hard not to laugh that I thought she was going to fall out of her chair. I tried to give her my most evil look. Danny, the clueless first grader just looked at it and then grinned. "It looks just like Uncle Albert's jacket. Cool!"

And then, just to prove that there was indeed justice in the world, Uncle Albert handed Claire her present. She got a sweater too. I guess there must have been a sale on yellow and green wool yarn, because hers was just like mine. And then Danny opened his. "Hey, we can be just like triplets." He actually put his on, and then Dad said, "Go ahead you two. Put yours on too. I'll get a picture. We can send it to

Aunt Beattie."

Great. Saved for all time.

We stood in front of the tree with Uncle Albert. All of us wore green and yellow so that we'd match. Uncle Albert and Danny were the ones who were smiling. I remember that Claire muttered under her breath about how green and yellow really looked good on me and maybe I should wear it on the first day back to school. Great idea. Just like having a big 'kick me' sign on my back. I won though. I told her that I thought I'd send a copy of the photo to her boyfriend. I could tell I'd gotten even when she mentioned later that if I did, I probably wouldn't live through the week.

Chapter 7

Christmas Gets Weird

And then came Uncle Albert's gifts. I know you were thinking that he'd brought the sweaters, but they were from Aunt Beattie, not him. He gathered us in front of the fireplace and took out this weird leather pouch that tied at the top. First, he explained that he didn't give the types of presents that children usually expected. His were different. "This bag is full of marbles," he said. "I want each of you to reach inside and very carefully select the best marble. Don't show anybody what it is until I tell you to. Now, who's going to go first?"

Ok. This was weird. Danny and I both looked at Claire. She was the oldest, so she should go first, but she wasn't about to put her hand into that strange pouch. I suppose she was worried that it might be filled with spiders or snakes or something. So I stepped up. "I will." I reached out my hand and boldly stuck it into the bag. It was full of marbles. No spiders. No snakes.

I swished around a little bit, and then pulled out one marble. "Remember," he said. "Don't show anybody yet."

So I went over to the couch and sat down. Mom wanted to look, but I held my hand closed. I didn't even look myself.

Danny chose next, and then Claire. Nobody looked. Suddenly, Christmas went from fun, well, except for the sweaters, to serious. After we were done, Uncle Albert set the bag down.

"OK, you may look."

I opened my hand. I had a big steel marble with a 'P' printed on it with some kind of permanent marker. Danny's had a 'C,' and Claire had a 'B.' Uncle Albert looked, and then nodded like he was some kind of old Indian wise man. "I couldn't have chosen better myself."

Dad looked over now. "What did you get?"

I just shrugged my shoulders. "Beats me. A marble with a 'P' on it."

"Hmm," he said.

Uncle Albert wasn't done yet though. "I suppose you want me to tell you what those letters mean."

Duh. Looks like a steel marble with a letter written on it to me. If it's something else, you'd better start talking. Well, that's what I thought. Actually, I just said, "Okay."

Then he launched into this long story about how a lost tribe of boys, probably the ones who taught him Mumblety Peg, had emerged from a forest where they'd lived with the animals for several years. They'd come to live in the small town where he grew up and he made friends with several of them. They told him about living alone in the forest with

35

no parents or other adults. I liked that part. They had to learn to fish, and hunt, and to identify edible berries and roots and other plants. They even learned how to make a bow and arrow, and snares, and lots of other cool stuff. The part I liked best was when Danny asked if they had a bedtime, or if they had to clean their closets. Nope. No parents to make them do anything. Then he took a long look at each of us.

"Much of what they learned came from the forest spirits, the spirits of long dead trees, and bears, and wolves, and even little squirrels." He paused for a second. "Animals are very wise, you know." He could tell that we didn't believe him, well, Claire didn't, and I wasn't sure. Danny was nodding like every word was true. Mom and Dad just looked worried. "Imagine if you got lost in the forest. Would you know what to eat? Where to find water? How to build a safe nest so that you could sleep without worrying about all the bigger animals who want to eat you?" Now I was a little worried. "Even a little squirrel knows those things. Do you?" He wagged his finger from side to side in front of us. "So never question the wisdom of forest animals. They know their own world even better than you know yours."

He stared at us for a minute, and then rocked his head back and forth and kind of nodded, before continuing. "The leader of all of the animals was a beautiful woman. My friends told me that she only appeared as a drifting column of smoke, and only at dusk when they were laying around their campfire, half asleep. 'Boys,' she would say, 'Sleep well tonight knowing that I and all of the others are protecting you, for you have important destinies ahead.'"

"Do you know what destiny means?" he asked.

I shook my head, but Claire said, "Kind of like what you're supposed to do."

"Exactly. What you're supposed to do." Then his eyes flared. It was really spooky, just like somebody lit a red candle in them. He went on, "But not just what you're supposed to do today, like wash the dishes or finish your homework. Your destiny is what you're supposed to do for your whole life." He leaned his head forward so that he was right in front of us. Even Mom and Dad looked a little spooked now. "The spirit of the smoke was a beautiful woman who watched over those boys even as she helped to guide their destinies. And she gave each of them a gift."

"What'd they get?" Danny asked.

Uncle Albert held out the pouch. "Marbles." Danny nodded, like that explained everything, but Claire kind of rolled her eyes and sat back with her arms crossed. Uncle Albert just smiled. "I didn't believe it myself, when I first heard their story, but it's true." He looked around, winked at us, and then said, "These aren't any ordinary marbles. These are marbles of destiny." The way he stretched out that last word made it sound really important. "Des---ti---ny."

"Right," Claire said, "So how'd you get the marbles?"

"Ah, you're wise to question. The oldest forest boy was Ike, and he and I got to be good friends." He looked at me. "Billy, you know how the sun seems to stay up forever in the summer?"

We all nodded, and he continued, "Well, Ike and I were sitting outside, taking turns swinging on an old rope that hung from a tree, when suddenly he said, I need to go. I hear her calling. I didn't hear anything, but it was getting dark out, and I knew he lived with his aunt, so I asked if that was who was calling."

Uncle Albert paused, shaking his head. "But it wasn't his aunt. Who do you suppose it was?"

"The smoke lady!" Danny said.

"That's right. The beautiful woman who only came out just before the boys fell asleep was calling him back into the forest. And just like that, he jumped off the rope swing and ran out through the trees. I didn't know what to do, should I stay there? Should I go inside and tell my mother? Or should I follow him?"

Claire and I just stared, but Danny shouted, "Follow him!"

"And so I did. He knew where he was going, but I didn't, so it was hard. Remember, it was dusk, and in the forest, it was getting darker and darker."

"Did you turn on your flashlight?" Danny asked.

"No flashlight. I just tried not to fall over roots, or run into tree trunks, but nothing seemed to want to get in my way. It was like I was supposed to follow. I heard my friend ahead of me, but he was quiet because he knew how to walk in the forest, so it was hard. Still, I followed and followed and followed. Finally, when I thought for sure that I was lost, and would have to spend the night fighting off bears and wolves, I saw a light ahead of me. I went slowly toward that light. It was the flickering of a campfire, and in the smoke, I saw the most beautiful woman I'd ever seen."

He paused, and Claire asked, "What did she look like?"

Now he smiled for the first time since he began the story. "I can't describe her. She was tall and slender, and then short and stout, but always beautiful and always changing and always enchanting. As soon as I emerged from the trees into the clearing, she called to me. Her voice was like bells ringing and songbirds singing. 'Albert,' she said, 'I'm so pleased that you could join us. Sit there, relax, and sleep later. I'll keep you safe tonight.'"

"And so I did. Ike was there, and Joe, one of the other forest boys, and Petie Raines was with them. It was like we'd been invited, and the forest boys were our escorts."

"Then the woman said, 'I wish to give you a gift, for you are the most special of all of the boys in your little village.' And then, just like magic, a leather bag appeared, right in front of me." He held up the bag full of marbles. "This leather bag." He swung his head from side to side, looking at each of us, and then said, "Then the woman told each of us to open the bag, reach in, and very carefully select the best marble in the bag. Each of us did, Petie, and Ike, and Joe, and me. Once we did, we had to hold the marble, not showing it to anyone until she gave us permission. But we all looked at our own. Mine had a 'W' on it."

He held out a marble in his hand for all of us to see. I just wondered where that had come from. It was metal, and rusted, and looked really old, but the 'W' still looked like it had been written the day before.

"This marble has been my destiny, and has guided my life ever since that day." He put it down on the coffee table in front of us. "And now you have a marble of destiny, just like mine, but more about that later. Let me finish my story. I don't remember falling asleep, but I do remember the lady of the smoke whispering in my ear that my destiny in life was to become a 'wanderer.' And that was true. I have spent my life wandering all over the world, sharing these wonderful marbles with children just like you." He picked up the marble off of the table, and looked at it. "There are many paths that a man, or a woman," he nodded at Claire, "can take in this life, and mine was right for me."

"Did you have to wander?" Danny asked.

"No," he said, and reached out to tussle his hair. "What you do with your life is your decision. The marble kind of pushes your destiny, but it doesn't decide it."

"Was the beautiful smoke lady still there when you woke up?"

"No. She vanished with the fire. We woke up just before daybreak, each of us was in our own bed with the covers drawn up, just like we'd slept there all night long. But each of us also carried home a bag of marbles and a mission to share them with other children who we felt were worthy."

Chapter 8

Marbles

We were all looking at his bag now. "How many marbles have you given away?" Claire finally asked.

Uncle Albert chuckled. "Many children are worthy, so I've given many marbles. I don't know how many."

"Don't you ever run out of marbles?" I asked.

He just shook his head.

"But where do they come from?"

He shrugged his shoulders, "The bag's never been empty." Then he said, "Look." He took a small box off of the floor and put it on the table. Then he handed me the marble bag. "Pour the marbles into that box."

I did. There were about two-dozen marbles, but none had letters on them. I picked one up and said, "Hey, there's no writing on these."

"Of course not," he said. "No child has selected them." He smiled and turned to Danny and Claire. "Don't take his word for it. Check them out."

They turned over marble after marble, but couldn't see any writing.

"There's nothing," Claire said.

Uncle Albert then asked me, "Did you get them all?"

"I think so." I checked the bag. It was empty. "Yeah."

He held out his hand. "Now, I want you to flatten out the bag, roll it up, and hand it to me."

I did, but as soon as I gave it to him, he said, "No, you need to take all the marbles out."

I was confused. "I did."

"I don't think so." He handed me back the bag. It was full of marbles!

"Whoa! How'd you do that?" I asked.

"I told you," he said. "For as long as I've had the marble bag, and for all of the marbles I've given away over many years, the bag has never been empty."

Then he cocked his head toward the table and we all looked. The box of marbles was just a box now. The marbles were gone. Whoa!

Even Dad was shocked at that one. "How'd you...you aren't even next to that table!"

"The smoke lady!" Danny said, his eyes wide.

Uncle Albert poured the marbles back into the box, and had us check them out while he stood over by the fireplace with the bag. There were no markings on any of the marbles. He tossed me the bag.

"Fill it back up," he said. Then he looked at Dad. "Go ahead, draw out a marble, but be very careful to select the best one. Tell me what it says."

Dad reached in and took out a marble. Then his eyes went wide, "But it didn't have any writing."

He looked over to Uncle Albert who nodded and said, "It does now, right?"

Dad stared down at it. "R."

Uncle Albert nodded. "I would have thought so." He looked toward my mother. "And you?"

I held out the bag for her. She took out one of the marbles. "It's an 'F.'"

He nodded again.

"So how did you get the letters on there?" Dad asked.

He just held up his hands. "I'm over here by the fireplace, nowhere near your marbles. Perhaps you should ask Billy. He has the bag."

"Don't look at me," I said.

"Would you like to know what the letters mean?"

Chapter 9

Destinies

We all nodded and leaned forward eagerly, looking at our marbles.

Uncle Albert sat again in Dad's favorite chair. "I don't usually give marbles to adults because your destinies are kind of set, but I thought today, with the questions, it might be a good idea." He looked at Dad. "You drew an 'R,' right?"

When Dad nodded, he said, "You will always be responsible, and I can see that in the way that you care for your family. You work hard, both at work and at home." Then he looked at Mom. "An 'F,' I believe. When she nodded, he said, "Ferocious."

Dad started to laugh, and Mom gave him a look I could only describe as ferocious. Uncle Albert went on, "You are ferocious in the defense of your family and what you think is right."

Dad was still laughing. "You got that right." Then he ducked when Mom threw a pillow at him.

"Now you three," Uncle Albert said. "Understand, as I know your parents do, that each of these destinies can be both positive and negative. Sometimes your father is too responsible, and he needs to learn to play. That's why I insisted on teaching him Mumblety Peg yesterday. As for your mother, some people don't understand that while she can be ferocious, she is also a good listener, a partner, and a fair judge." I saw my parents nodding.

"Claire, you drew a 'B.' That stands for Beauty, and not just physical beauty, but beauty of heart and soul. People want to be near you, because it makes them feel better about themselves. Beware though, that sometimes you can get a little full of yourself, and push others away with hurtful comments."

Claire looked down at the marble in her hand, nodding as if she understood exactly what he meant.

He continued, "Danny, you drew a 'C.' That stands for Curiosity. That's a wonderful trait to have. People with curiosity solve problems sometimes before others even know that they're there. All of our great scientists and engineers and doctors and leaders and teachers are curious. The challenge for you is to remember that curiosity killed the cat. Don't go sticking your hands into a fire just because you're curious about how hot it is."

He looked at me then. "Billy, you drew a 'P.' You have Presence." He saw me frown, and then chuckled. "No, not presents, presence. People want to please you. They ask you questions and follow you. When you enter a room, people know that someone important has just come in, even before they see you. Beware though, that even the greatest leaders sometimes go in the wrong direction.

45

Don't be afraid to change if you see that you're making a mistake."

He looked at us all. "And that is my gift to you. Follow your destinies. Use what you know about yourselves and your special gifts to guide your pleasures while you help others. And now," he took back the marble bag and stood up. "I'm going to follow my destiny and take a nap." He winked. "Maybe I'll dream about some fantastic journey." He pointed at Danny and then at me with a playful scowl on his face. "These boys woke me up at four. They're not particularly quiet on Christmas morning."

Chapter 10

Good Bye

We took Uncle Albert to the train station the next morning. He was all dressed up for his trip in his yellow and green check jacket, yellow shoes, stained white shirt and paisley bow tie. Mom asked him why he didn't wear the new shirt.

"What? And ruin it? I'm going to save that for a special occasion. It's my best looking shirt. Those train stewards will probably just pour coffee on it."

And then it was time for the goodbyes. We all said thank you for the marbles, but I'm not sure why. I mean, it was a fun story and all that, and he's a heck of a magician, but really? Marbles that give special powers? Only Danny still believed everything was true, but what can you expect from a first grader. He even believed Mom when he caught her putting a quarter under his pillow after he lost a tooth. She told him that the tooth fairy had dropped it on the floor and she was just picking it back up. I mean, really!

Still, he was an interesting old coot. That's what Dad called him, not me, but it seemed to fit.

So there we were, standing on the platform at the train station, ready to send him off to Portland where he was visiting some other relatives we didn't even know we had. I asked Dad about that. He told me that it was all in the family tree. You get first cousins. Those are the kids you play with when your aunts and uncles come over and bring their families. Then you get to second cousins. Those are the ones from your grandparents' brothers and sisters, and they're kind of related, but not really, and you probably don't see much of them. Then you get as old as Uncle Albert, and you have third and fourth cousins. You could be walking down the street and pass your third cousin and not even know who they are! How crazy is that?

It's kind of like the family trees and charts they set up in science class, where they show how different animals all came from a common ancestor millions of years ago. You've seen them, where they show that if you go back far enough, we're related to chimpanzees.

Of course, Dad couldn't leave it at that. He wanted me to know that I might have just eaten my three millionth cousin Fred for breakfast this morning when I had bacon. Ol' Fred's family went on to be pigs while my ancestors decided to be people. Did I tell you my family was strange?

Anyway, Uncle Albert was leaving on the train, and I was getting my bed back. Mom said she'd change the sheets later today. I suggested that she might want to change the mattress too, but she just gave me a funny look. You can tell she never came into the room in the middle of the night. I tried to talk her into at least washing the mattress pad, because it smelled like Uncle Albert, and you know what she said? I mean, who could have predicted this? She said, "You're no bed of roses yourself, Billy."

I mean, how could she compare clean boy scent with gross old man stench? It was unbelievable. If Uncle Albert comes back, I think it's Claire's turn. She can sleep under the desk while he stinks up her room.

Uncle Albert suggested that we all wear our new sweaters to the train station so that we could get a picture of the family in front of the train, but thank goodness it was warm out. Danny still wore his, but he's a first grader. 'Nuff said.

After the train pulled out, Dad said, "Well that was interesting."

Mom just laughed. Then she decided we should hurry home so that we could all start writing thank you letters. Boy was I looking forward to that, especially the one to Aunt Beattie for the sweater. I figured that if I was really lucky, it'd never be cold enough to wear it this winter. By next winter, I'll be able to give it to Danny.

Chapter 11

Presence

That night, I was laying in bed, really enjoying my super comfortable mattress, and glad that I could sit up in the middle of the night without whacking my head on the desk, and trying to keep from gagging on old man smell. And then my mind started wandering. You know, how you're not really asleep, but you're kind of dreaming anyway? I was thinking about this whole marble thing, like what if there was something to it after all. It's true that Dad's responsible, but I just figured it was because he was Dad. It's the way he is. And I remember when Mom was babysitting Susie Pritchard back when she and Danny were in preschool, and Susie bit Danny on the arm. Mom just smacked her. She didn't tell her to stop, or give her any warning. She just smacked her. Then she was kind of sorry about it, and said it was just a reaction and tried to make sure Susie was OK, and apologized to Susie's mom. But she was still ferocious, even if Susie's mom said "No problem. Susie knows not to bite."

So like I said, there I was, laying in bed, thinking about

marbles, and presence, and then I started to dream. I was going to a birthday party, and we were late because Danny wouldn't take off his yellow and green checkerboard sweater, so I went running in to the house and everything stopped, and then Paul came over and said, "Billy, I'm glad you made it." And then before I could say anything, he turned around and said, "Ok everybody. We can start the party now. Billy's here." It was weird. When I walked into the family room, they were all studying their multiplication tables, but when they saw me, they all jumped up and cheered and decided to play pin the tail on the donkey. I don't remember whose birthday it was. I gave him a bag of marbles.

Chapter 12

Presence Two

You ever have one of those dreams where you're flying?
Like you can run, and if you run fast enough, you just start
soaring out way above the ground? I had one of those last
night. It was a cool dream, and I really liked it until the
end, when Uncle Albert came flying up next to me and said
it was time for me to meet the smoke lady. That part was a
little strange, but it was okay. And then he started spurting
ahead of me, like he was jet propelled, and had to keep
coming back. "Sorry," he said, "I had beans for lunch."

He was right about the smoke lady though. She was really
beautiful and wispy. She kind of danced with the smoke,
waving back and forth. I was there with Paul and all of my
friends from fourth grade, and everyone said later that it
was like she was looking right at them. And then she
drifted over to me and held out a smoky hand and said,
"Take this, Billy. It's your destiny." It was a silver metal
marble with a 'P' on it. I put it in my pocket just before I
woke up.

A lot of weird things happened in January, after I went back to school, and I had to wonder if they had anything to do with the whole presence thing.

First, Mrs. McKenzie started calling on me more in class, like she just wanted to know what I had to say, which was usually nothing more than I had before. And then, she'd rub her chin sometimes and say, "Hmm. Interesting answer." What's that suppose to mean? In fact, one day she called on Rosie S., and then, just when Rosie S. was about to answer, she said, "No, I think I want to hear from Billy on this instead. Sorry, Rosie S."

And then there was soccer. My school was going to have a game against Willow Heights Elementary, so we were all practicing with the PE teacher. And he seemed to catch me every time I fouled somebody, even when I did it by accident. It wasn't fair at all. A couple of the guys were just about pounding on the other team, but did they get called? No. Never. Just Billy, the guy Coach Ed seemed to be watching constantly.

And then there was the day that Danny was being a real pest. I was out in the back yard with Paul and Ricky and Craig building a fort. We had an old pile of cinder blocks out there, left over from building the house, and we'd rearrange them every couple of months into a new fort. And do you think we could get rid of Danny? No way. He was always there. I even went to Mom and tried to get her to keep him inside, but she was no help. "He's your brother," she said. "Let him play with you." So we included him a little, but that wasn't enough. Craig and Ricky were putting up parapets on top, using sticks sticking straight up on top of the cinder blocks, just to make the fort a little higher, when Danny came running through and knocked everything down. They were really mad. We all were, so we chased him off. Then Craig said we needed to do something to get back at him, and we decided to haul his bicycle up into the tree where he couldn't get it. Who do you suppose got in trouble for that? That's right. Me. It wasn't even my idea! I just got in trouble because he was my brother and I should have known better. But I did know better.

It was because of my presence. I got noticed for good things, but I also got noticed when things went bad. Some gift!

Chapter 13

Back To Sixth Grade

Remember that I started this story telling about how I had a problem? Yeah, I almost forgot too, but that presence stuff was pretty important, so I figured I'd better let you know about it.

Anyway, there I was. I'd just dropped off the attendance roster to Mrs. Madigan in the office when she said, "So what do you think we should do, Billy?"

How should I know? Mr. Johnson was acting really strange, I could tell that.   He was in his principal office, but something was definitely wrong with him.

"Why's he doing that?" I asked.

"You mean the singing and the dancing and the summersaults?"

"Yeah," like I would mean anything else.

"He was at it when I came in at seven. He's been doing it ever since."

Wow. Our principal was nuts. I can understand singing, but the Oscar Meyer Wiener song over and over and over? And break dancing? And turning summersaults? And all this while he was dressed up in a clown outfit? "Is he practicing for a talent show or something?"

She just shook her head. "This happens every once in a while, but usually it only lasts for a few minutes, and then he shakes his head, like he's waking up, and goes back to being Mr. Johnson. It's never lasted this long."

So our principal's finally lost it, and not just a little bit, but a lot. "Maybe I should go talk to him," I said. She smiled, so I went over to his office, and peeked through the door just as he rolled across the floor into the doorway and ran into my feet. He looked up. I looked down.

"Ah, Billy," he said as he bounced up. Bounced up? Mr. Johnson? This guy was just barely younger than Uncle Albert. What got into him?

"Uh, Hi Mr. Johnson. You okay?"

"Never better," he said, but it came out more like "Nnnneeeevvvveeeerrrr beeeettteeeerrrr," since he was in the middle of a back flip. He landed on his hands, and then just stayed there, walking over to me upside down. Then he started to sing. "Oh, I wish I was an Oscar Meyer Wiener, That is what I'd really like to be e e." Then he flipped back to his feet, grabbed a towel, and wiped the sweat off of his forehead. "So what do you think, Billy? You like my act?"

His act? What, flipping around and singing a stupid song in his office? But it seemed like a serious question. "Uh..."

"Come on, I'm trying to make it better. What do you think?"

"Uh, I didn't know you could do handstands or flips."

"Oh, that. Well, I used to be a gymnast back in college. It's been a few years, but I think I've still got it."

A few years? Like Uncle Albert had a few wrinkles? I checked out my principal. His hair was completely white. It had been white since I was in kindergarten. And he wasn't a skinny man. If my grandpa had a potbelly, Mr. Johnson was shaped more like a barrel. He was right about one thing though. Whatever 'it' was, he had it. I just hoped it wasn't contagious. I asked the only question I could think of. "Uh, what are you doing?"

"Rehearsing," he said, and then started summersaulting around the room while he sang. Finally, he stood up. "I'm going to try out for a new TV show, America's Most Amazing Acts."

OK. Amazing wasn't quite the word I'd use to describe a fat old man doing back flips and summersaults while singing the Oscar Meyer Wiener song. Strange maybe, or disgusting. I tried to get him to sit in his chair. "Don't you feel like sitting down for a couple of minutes? Just to get some rest?"

He did another back flip, and then walked over to me on his hands. "Not right now... Oscar Meyer Wiener... gotta practice." Then he flipped upright again and that's when things turned really weird.

"Speaking of which, I'm flying to Hollywood tonight. I'll be gone for a couple of days, so I thought that since you're the student council president, you should take over."

WHAT????

Ok. Let me get this straight. I was the student council president, one of those presence things where most people in the school knew me, so they voted for me. So far, my job had been to introduce people at assemblies, like the guy who brought the raven and the porcupine and the beaver, or the guy who blew up balloons filled with different gasses. That was pretty awesome, by the way, and really, really loud. Or, I'd lead the student council meetings with Mrs. Kinney's help. Now I was supposed to be in charge of the entire school?

Part of me was jumping up and down in circles inside. I mean, was this the coolest thing that ever happened to a kid or what? I would be in charge for a couple of days. No homework, that'd be the first thing to go, and forget about the ban on tackle football. Tomorrow we'd be playing like the pros. The ideas were endless.

On the other hand, I had this little warning bell dinging inside of my head, telling me that this could be disastrous. I didn't know how, it was something that my gut was trying to tell me. But did I listen? Noooooo.

I looked up at Mr. Johnson. "Ok. When do I start?"

"That's the attitude," he said with a bounce onto his desk. "I knew I could count on you. How about right now? I need to get home to pack."

"Uhhhhhh?" I could feel my jaw drop. "Now, like in right now?"

"Sure. You're ready, aren't you?"

And before I could stop him, he was picking up his briefcase and heading out into the hallway. "Oh, one more thing," he said over his shoulder just as he opened the front door to the office, "I left you a list of things to do on my desk. See ya in a couple of days!" And then he was gone.

And there I was, Billy Rader, sixth grader, Student Council President ………….. and Principal.

Chapter 14

The List

I went over to his desk. The list was in a brown folder, with a post-it note on top that said, 'Things for Billy.'

So he had planned this whole thing in advance? Wow. I opened it up. There was a thick file of papers inside. The first one, right on the top, said,

DO NOT, UNDER ANY CIRCUMSTANCES

NOT EVEN IF THERE'S AN EMERGENCY

NOT EVEN IF YOU DON'T KNOW WHAT TO DO

NOT EVEN IF YOUR MOM SHOWS UP AND YOU HAVE TO GO TO THE DENTIST BECAUSE ALL OF YOUR TEETH FELL OUT.

DO NOT TELL THE SUPERINTENDENT

WHERE I'VE GONE.

Ok. I guess that was pretty clear, though I kind of hoped that part about all my teeth falling out wouldn't really happen. I'd end up looking just like Grandpa Jake after he dumped his false teeth in the jar before going to bed, and that wasn't a pretty sight. I turned to the next page. It said that he'd scheduled an assembly for 11:00 to tell the kids and the teachers that he'd be gone for a couple of days and I'd be in charge. Well, that seemed like a good idea. Or at least it sounded like it would help. After all, that way the kids would know before lunch that the principal was gone, and I'd be supervising lunch in the multipurpose room, along with the lunch ladies.

Then I turned to the next page. Sammy Franco's parents were coming right after school at 3:00 to meet with the principal and Sammy and his teacher. It said that Sammy wasn't following the class rules. I had to laugh out loud at that. I knew Sammy. He was one of Danny's buddies, and I'd heard stories of some of the stuff he did in class. Most of it was kind of funny, at least to Danny, but I guess Sammy's teacher didn't think so. He'd been over to the house a few times too and yeah, I could see why she'd think he was a little twerp.

I looked at the next page. This one was way better. I got to give out the good effort awards. Two or three kids in each class whose teachers thought they were working especially hard were nominated for effort awards each month. Mr. Johnson went to every classroom and gave out pencils with the school name on them. Easy, fun, and cool.

The next page was some kind of order packet for school supplies. The note said, "Have Mrs. Madigan help you to order the school supplies for next month. You can sign the bottom with my signature stamp. You'll find that in my top desk drawer." I glanced through the list. Most of it was paper, and pencils, and pens, and art supplies. There was also a list of supplies for teachers, like staplers and hole punches. When I looked further, I found protractors and compasses, like the ones we used in math, when our partners finished with them because there were never enough. Guess I'd solve that problem, at least for my class. The last pages in the packet were all science supplies. I came to one entry. 'Fetal Pig,' and underneath it, 'Scalpel,' sixth grade only. I knew that a scalpel was a knife like a doctor used, but what was a fetal pig?

I carried the list out to Mrs. Madigan and showed it to her. "What's a fetal pig?" I asked.

"Oh, we haven't ordered those in years. Students used to dissect them to learn about body parts."

"You mean cut them up to see the guts and stuff?"

She nodded. "That's right. They'd work in teams with the science teacher. But that was before Mr. Wallace left."

"Hmm. Thanks." I went back into Mr. Johnson's office. I remembered Mr. Wallace. He called himself Mr. Science, and was really a lot of fun, but he'd blown up the science classroom and had to move to another school when I was in second grade. I took out one of Mr. Johnson's pencils and wrote 20 on the order form. After all, we had 64 sixth graders, and we worked in teams of four, plus a few extras just in case. I could hardly wait to tell the guys that we were going to get to cut up fetal pigs and see their guts!

I'd just filled in a few other things that I figured we needed in sixth grade when Mrs. Madigan poked her head into the office. "Billy?"

Uh oh. I'd been caught in Mr. Johnson's office. Suddenly, my blood turned cold and I began to sweat. Then I thought, wait, I have permission to be here. Still, I felt kind of nervous. Wouldn't you if you got caught writing on an order sheet in the principal's office. I turned around. "What?"

Chapter 15

Max

"I've got a couple of third graders out here. Their teacher sent them in for fighting."

Uh, so what was I supposed to do about that? Yell at them? Threaten to take away every recess until they were old enough to go to middle school? "Uh, give me a minute, okay?"

She just looked at me for a while and I could tell she was thinking, 'so what am I supposed to do with them while you're twiddling your thumbs?' Then she shrugged her shoulders. "Fine. One minute."

I could tell by the way she said it that she didn't want it to turn into two minutes or even a minute and a half. She left, and I thought quickly. What did Mom do when Danny and I got into a fight? Listen to both sides. Try and figure out what really happened. Give a consequence. But I couldn't really send them to their room, could I? Yeah, but I could make them pick up garbage during recess. That always needed to be done, and it was one of Mr. Johnson's favorite punishments. We kids hated it.

I walked out, looked at the two third graders, and put on my sternest face. "Ok, you two, come with me."

I didn't recognize either of them, even though they were in Danny's grade. One of them said, "Yeah? Who are you?"

He was probably right. They had expected to see Mr. Johnson. "I'm Billy Rader. Mr. Johnson isn't here right now. He asked me to cover for him." The boy looked at his enemy and just shrugged. They followed me into the office.

Once they got there, I made them stand while I sat down. That's what my dad did when we got into a fight at home. We hated it. "Ok. You first." I pointed to the boy nearest the door. "What's your name?"

"Uh, Johnny, Johnny Toft."

I wrote it down and pointed to the other. "And you?" He was a surly little worm. He just looked at the floor and kicked his feet. "Hey," I said. "I didn't hear you? What's your name?"

Then he stuck his head up defiantly, "None of your business."

Hmm. This I hadn't expected. If I ever said that to my parents, my butt would be so bruised I wouldn't be able to sit down for days. But I wasn't born yesterday. I turned to the other fighter. "What's his name?"

The other kid smiled for the first time. "Michael, and he started it."

I figured that was probably true, but maybe I should listen first. I wrote down his name on my paper. "Ok, Johnny, you want to tell me what happened?"

Johnny started to speak, but then Michael cast him a malicious look. "Uh, we got in a fight."

"Yeah, I know that. And your teacher sent you to the office. What started the fight."

Again the look from Michael, and Johnny said, "I don't know."

Hmm. Now what? "Okay Michael, what started the fight?"

"What fight?"

I threw my hands up in the air. "What do you mean what fight? Your teacher sent you here for fighting. Johnny just admitted that."

"I don't remember any fight." Then he sneered over at Johnny. "And he don't neither."

Johnny went pale, and stuttered, "He's r r r right. I d d don't."

And so I made my first decision as acting principal. I said, "Johnny, go see Mrs. Madigan. She'll give you a pass back to class. You get to sit at table eight during lunch."

He frowned and got up, and tried one last shot. "But I didn't do nothin'!"

"Ah," I said with a smile. My dad taught me this one. "If you didn't do nothin', then you must have done something."

He turned and left the room, looking confused. I guess they hadn't taught the grammar of double negatives in third grade yet.

By the way, does your school have a table eight? The reason why I ask is because I don't know. I mean, I've never been to your school. At my school, if you get in trouble, you have to sit at table eight for lunch with all of the other bad kids. You can't eat with your friends, or even talk, and you get dismissed to go play last. Nobody likes table eight.

But I can't take all my time talking about table eight. After all, I still had Michael standing in front of me, trying to scare me with his nastiest look. Guess he forgot who was the sixth grader and who was the third grader, and who could pound the other one with one hand tied behind his back. Speaking of which... I turned to him and gave him my own evil look. "You get table eight too, but first, I want you to sit on the floor here for a while."

"Yeah? Well what if I refuse? Whatcha gonna do about that?"

This kid was starting to get on my nerves. I held up a finger. "Just a minute." Then I walked out to Mrs. Madigan. She looked up from her work and I whispered, "Can you call Max Trestman's classroom? I need to talk to him."

Her eyes widened, and I knew just exactly why. Max had a reputation. "You want Max?"

"Yeah. It won't take long."

I turned back into the office. The kid was still standing

there, trying to bore holes in me with his eyes. I just laughed, "Yeah, yeah, yeah. It might work for third graders, but you don't even know who you're dealing with, buddy."

We stayed like that for a couple of minutes, in some kind of weird stare down contest, which by the way, I won, when Mrs. Madigan snuck a worried look around the door. "He's here."

"Good," I said, still staring at the little twerp across the office. "Send him in."

When Max walked in, the other kid seemed to shrink back. See, you've got to understand Max. He's not very smart, but he's a really big kid, even if he is only in fifth grade. In fact, I'll bet he weighs more than my dad. And he has kind of a reputation for fighting. And best of all, he's never lost a fight in his life, probably because he's a dirty fighter. He'll punch and wrestle, just like all the boys, but he also bites and lots of other nasty stuff. At least he used to. He hasn't really been in a fight in the last couple of years, because he's tired of everyone thinking he's mean. But nobody really knows that except for me and a few others, so he still has a bad rep. Anyway, best of all, I've been tutoring him in math since I was in fourth grade and he was in fifth grade for the first time. Hey, maybe that's why he's so big. This is his third trip through fifth grade. So anyway, Max likes me, because I help with his math, and he'll do just about whatever I ask him to do. And boy was I going to ask a favor now.

"Hey Max," I said.

"Hey Billy," he said.

"Max, I've got a little problem and I thought I'd ask for your help." This was a first. I never asked Max for help, so he was excited.

"Sure," he said. "Whatever you need, you got it."

I looked over at Michael. I think he was trying to file himself on Mr. Johnson's bookshelf. In fact, I could just imagine him under 'W' for worm.

"This kid here," I pointed to Michael, "He got in a fight this morning with one of the other boys in his classroom, and well, Mr. Johnson had to go out of town for a couple of days so he kind of left me in charge."

Max just nodded. I guess he didn't see anything wrong with me being principal. Then he said, "Where's the other kid?"

"He gets table eight."

"Yeah. Good. How about this one?"

"Well, he's being a little difficult. He threatened the other kid right here in the office in front of me. And he's been giving me a lot of lip about what am I going to do about it. That's not right, is it?"

Max shook his head and looked at the kid, like he was memorizing his face for that time after school when he'd need to know just who was scheduled for a good pounding.

I turned to the kid. I think now he was trying to do his best imitation of a bookmark inside of the 'Worm' books on the bookshelf. "You didn't really mean to do that, did you?"

The kid shook his head from side to side so violently that I thought it might break loose and fly off. "No sir. I'm really sorry. I'll never do that again."

"And you're never going to fight with anybody again, are you? Because if you do, I'm going to have to call on Max."

Just in case the kid didn't get it, Max pounded one huge fist into his open palm, making a loud smack. The kid just about jumped out of his shoes. "No. No more fighting."

"And no fighting on the way to school or on the way home either, right? I wouldn't want to hear from Johnny that you were waiting for him after school today."

"No. Never again. I'm really really really really really sorry."

"Good." I smiled. "I'm glad you see things that way." I hesitated for a minute. "I still think there should be some kind of consequence though." I turned to Max. "What do you think?"

Max ground his fist into his palm, and raised his eyebrows while he growled at the kid. "Yeah."

Now I thought the kid was about to pee his pants, and I didn't think Mr. Johnson would like it if some kid peed in his office, so I said, "How about table eight and garbage pickup at lunchtime? That sound fair to you Max?"

"Yeah."

That's one of the things I liked about Max. A man of few words. The kid breathed a sigh of relief I'm sure they heard all the way back in his classroom. I looked at Michael. "How about you?"

"Sure Billy. Thanks for being so fair."

"That's all then, I think," I said. "See you at lunchtime. And you're going to make sure you pick up lots of garbage, aren't you."

The kid jerked his head, up and down this time. "Everything out there."

"Good," I said. "Well, I guess we're about done here. You can pick up your note from Mrs. Madigan."

You know those cartoon characters on TV whose legs go so fast when they run that you can't even see them? This kid was faster.

I turned to Max. "Thanks buddy. We still on for tomorrow after school?"

"Yeah," he groaned. "Fractions."

"Don't forget that you'll need a note from Mrs. Madigan too. See you at lunch."

After Max left, I leaned back in Mr. Johnson's chair, hands behind my head. Heck yeah, I could do this. It was going to be a snap.

I couldn't have been more wrong.

Chapter 16

The Assembly

I stood at the front of the multipurpose room, watching as all of the kids filed in, one class at a time, single file, the little kids toward the front and the bigger kids at the back. The lunch tables had all been pushed against the walls, and the sixth graders got to sit on the benches. Everyone else was on the floor. Well, everybody except for the teachers. They all got chairs. I always figured that was so that they'd be high enough over the kids to see who was messing up. And probably because they're so old that it's hard for them to get back up from the floor, too.

We started at 11:05, just after the last of the kids settled into place. I'd asked the student council officers to come up to the front with me, so they were on the stage too, along with Mrs. Madigan.

I walked out to the center of the stage, where Joe, our custodian, had set up the microphone. The kids were used to seeing me there, since I introduced the assemblies, and had been the master of ceremonies for the fall talent show. "Good morning," I said in a loud voice. Then I pumped my fist and yelled, "Go Tigers!"

Tigers are our school mascot. We have drawings of Tigers on the bulletin boards, and on the sign out front, and on every kid's folder that they get at the beginning of the year. A few kids mumbled, "Go Tigers."

I repeated myself even louder, "I didn't hear you. I said, Go Tigers." Now the kids yelled, especially the little ones at the front.

"Much better," I said. Then I called Mrs. Madigan to the stage. I figured that everyone knew the school secretary, and having her there would make it seem like I really might have been appointed as the principal, and that I had her approval.

Ok. Here goes, I thought as I stood next to her. "Mr. Johnson scheduled this assembly to let you know that he'll be out of town for a couple of days."

I heard one of the kids along the side say, "All Right!" It seemed to come from my class, so I looked over and shook my head. Time to get it over. "So, since I'm the Student Council President, he asked me to fill in for him." There it was. Everybody in the school, except for Max and the two third graders was hearing the news at the same time. For a long time, maybe it was just a few seconds, but it seemed like it might be an hour, nobody said anything. Then the buzzing started, kind of like everyone was talking to somebody else, all at once. Most of the kids were smiling, even if they looked a little confused. Most of the teachers were frowning. My teacher, Mr. Ward, just kind of scowled, like he thought I should be sitting at my desk in his classroom, writing an essay on the periodic table or something.

I waited for just a little longer, and the buzz settled down, so I tapped the mic a couple of times to get everyone's attention and gave the quiet signal. I saw lots of kids hands go up to give the same signal, and almost all of the talking stopped. "I guess that's about it. Everything else will be the same, and Mr. Johnson should be back in a couple of days. Any questions?"

Several hands went up. I called on one of the second graders. "Where'd he go?"

I remembered that he didn't want the superintendent to know, so just in case this kid was some kind of spy, I just said, "Out of town, an emergency of some kind."

"Oh." He looked around.

I called on another one, a fifth grader. "We still having school lunch today?"

"Sure. Everything will be the same."

I pointed to a kindergartener. "My daddy went on a business trip to New York last week."

"Good. Is he back now?"

"Yeah. He brought me a T-shirt." Suddenly about twenty kindergarten and first grade hands shot up. I knew what that meant. They all had a story to tell. Little kids have trouble telling the difference between questions and stories.

I pointed to one of the kids sitting on the benches. He was in my class. "What's your question, Matt?"

"You get to suspend kids?"

I hadn't thought about that, and I guess I could have

counted on Matt to bring it up. "I don't know. I guess. He told me I was going to do his job for a couple of days. He didn't tell me I couldn't."

"Oh," he leaned back, a little nervous now.

I looked around the room. Lots of hands were still up, but I knew that we could spend the whole day with these questions. I decided to send them back. I remembered Mr. Johnson's line. "Okay. If you have any more questions, I'll be here at lunchtime. Look to your teacher to go back to class."

And suddenly, every teacher stood, and all the kids started talking. Well, I thought, that went well. I thanked the Student Council kids and followed Mrs. Madigan back to the office.

Chapter 17

Lunch

By now, I was starting to get hungry, and was looking forward to lunch. After all, I'd missed out on recess in the morning, and hadn't even had a snack. So I walked back to my classroom and grabbed my book bag off of the back of my chair. The other kids, and my teacher all just stared at me, like I was some kind of three-eyed green skinned alien from the planet Zyrton or somewhere, but nobody said anything, so I just took my lunch and walked back to the office.

Once I got there, I put my lunch on Mr. Johnson's desk and then reached into the zipper pocket inside. Ah, the cell phone I'd gotten as a sixth grade present from my parents. It was supposed to be just for the times when I decided to go to somebody's house after school, or emergencies, and I wasn't ever supposed to take it out during class, but it also had a good music collection, and I was the principal, so I put in the ear buds and turned on the tunes. Then I leaned back in his chair. Yeah. I could do this.

I took a look at the rest of the folder he'd left me. It was more of the same stuff, a couple of meetings with parents, and an appointment with Mrs. Allistair, the president of the PTA. I didn't see any real problems.

Just before noon, I took my lunch and went to the multipurpose room. The little kids were due in there first. Then they'd go out and play while the big kids ate. And I figured that since I was hungry, and I had to be with both groups of kids during lunch, I might as well eat with the younger ones. I got to the doorway and looked in. The first classes were coming into the lunch line and going to their tables. The lunch supervisors were all spread out, looking ferocious, like any kid who did anything wrong was going to regret it for a long time. It only took about ten minutes for everyone to have lunch and be sitting. At first, I leaned against the stage, not quite knowing what to do. I guess it's because I could picture Mr. Johnson leaning against the stage too, eating his sandwich. Then I started to wander around. And it was really cool. The little kids were all excited that I was their principal and everybody wanted me to sit and eat at their table, so I sat down with a group of second graders.

And I had a great time! The lunchroom ladies took care of everybody, so even though I was supposed to supervise, there really wasn't anything for me to do except talk about second grade stuff.

They wanted to know what it was like being principal, and if I'd had a chance to yell at any kids yet. I told them I'd had to talk with a couple of boys in third grade and one said, "Oh yeah, Johnny and Michael. They were in a fight before school." Everybody nodded and the kid said, "Do they get table eight?"

And then they wanted to know what else I got to do. I couldn't think of much. I told them I had a couple of meetings with parents later, and had to supervise the big kids for lunch, and that I got to order school supplies and stuff.

Then one of the girls asked a really interesting question. "Can you get the teachers in trouble too?"

Well, I thought it was interesting. I'll bet you do too. I mean, we've all been in classrooms where teachers definitely needed somebody to come in and holler at them from time to time. I started to think about Mrs. Mckenzie, my fourth grade teacher and how mean she was, and what I could do to her. It made for an interesting lunch.

At 12:20, the kids went out to play and the fourth, fifth, and sixth grade teachers came in with the older kids. I was back at the front, leaning against the stage, doing my best to look like I did this every day. Paul and a couple of other guys were the first to come over. "So dude, you're the boss, eh?"

"I guess. For a couple of days anyway."

"So can you get me a pass to get out of homework for the rest of the week?"

Alan was with him, and he said, "Yeah, and ice cream for dessert after lunch."

They all laughed. Then Paul said, "So what did you do all morning?"

I just shrugged my shoulders. "Not much. I had to talk with a couple of third graders who were fighting, and work on the supply order, but that was about it."

They were all curious. "So what'd you do with the third graders?"

I just smiled. "Told one of them that if he kept getting in fights, I'd sic Max on him."

Their eyes widened. Even sixth graders were afraid of Max, but I guess that made sense. He was really supposed to be in seventh grade. "Really," Alan said. Then he shook his head. "I'd swear off fighting right there."

I laughed. "He did." I told them I thought poor Michael was about to pee his pants right there in Mr. Johnson's office and they all laughed. Then the lunch lady came over and shooed them over to their table. Since these were the older kids, I figured I'd do what Mr. Johnson did, and wander around more, just to make sure they were all following the lunch room rules. You know, no throwing trash on the floor, no making a mess with food, that kind of stuff. It didn't take long until it was time for them to go out and play too. As I watched the last of the kids to go out, I reflected that it had been a pretty good day so far.

Then I decided I could use some playtime too. Since I was principal though, I did it differently, and joined a fourth grade basketball game. Talk about fun, I was the tallest kid on the court, so they kept tossing the ball to me for layups. Since my team was winning big, I switched teams and helped the other guys to catch up, and then switched again, and again. Wow did I get a workout!

After lunch, I figured the day was about over, so I went back to Mr. Johnson's office. Two fifth graders were waiting for me there. I knew both of them by reputation. They'd been tossing carrots at each other during lunch, and the lunch lady had sent them in. I told them not to do that any more, assigned them to table eight for lunch on the next day, and sent both of them back to class. What a cake job!

Then I picked up the effort pencils and went out to deliver them. The kindergarten kids were the most fun. Their teachers got them all whipped up into a frenzy of excitement, and they cheered the winner in each class. By the time I got to sixth grade, the kids were a little more savvy. They still clapped and all, but weren't really excited about me interrupting art and science. After all, they'd figured out by then, that it was just a pencil, even if it was shiny and red, and had the school name on it.

The meeting with Sammy Franco's parents was easy. They promised to check to make sure he did his homework, and his teacher told them she'd send home a note every day to let them know how he was doing in class. Everyone except for Sammy seemed to agree that it was a good result.

And then it was time to go home. What a day!

Chapter 18

That Night

Danny spilled the beans at dinner. I'd gone out to play football at the park by Paul's house with some friends after school, and by the time I got home it was time to do homework before dinner. Oh yeah, I almost forgot about that. Mr. Ward stopped by the office with a package of work for me to do right after school got out. I was sure happy that he hadn't forgotten about me. What a guy. So as soon as I got home, I had to get busy with all the work from the day and all of the homework. I figured I could finish some of it in Mr. Johnson's office in the morning, but just in case, I wanted most of it to be done. So I completely forgot to mention my new job to anyone before dinner. Then I had to set the table and feed Walter, our dog, so I totally forgot. I could trust Danny though.

My father always sits at the head of the table, and my mother at the opposite end, with Danny and me on one side and Claire across from us. Dad started the conversation as usual. "How was school today?"

Claire didn't even look up from her food. Mom said she

was going through some kind of phase where she was embarrassed by everything her family did, like asking how school was. I, on the other hand, didn't even know where to start. Danny solved the problem. He stuffed his mouth full of green beans and then said, "Billy's the new principal," only it came out kind of like "brgh a n prpl."

"Remember," Dad said, "You shouldn't talk with your mouth full. Nobody can understand you. Chew your food and swallow and then tell us what you said." Danny chewed, swallowed, and then took a drink of milk. Then he said, "Billy's the new principal."

My father looked at me. My mother looked at me. Claire laughed so loud that she snorted milk out of her nose and asked to excuse herself. Danny looked offended that they didn't believe him. "It's true," he insisted, "Billy's the new principal."

"Billy?" my father said, "Something you forgot to mention?"

Uh oh, that was the way he acted when he knew I was in trouble for something before I knew he knew about it. "Uh, yeah. Mr. Johnson's gone for a couple of days so since I'm student council president, he asked me to take over for him."

My father just stared at me, his jaw open. If it had been me looking that way, he'd have told me to close my mouth before the flies flew in.

Claire was back by now, and she just said, "Yeah. Right. My doufus brother has been appointed as the principal. What happened, they run out of smart kids to do the job?"

As you can see, I can always count on my sister to stick up for me. "No, milk snot, they didn't. I was the first choice."

My mother raised her hand up. "Enough, you two." She looked at me, curious. "So, uh, what did you do today?"

"Well, we had an assembly, so I was there for that, and then I supervised lunch, and met with some parents, and..." I hesitated. What else did I do? "Oh yeah, I sent in the supply order. Mr. Johnson gave me his signature stamp so that I could order anything I wanted."

"Right," Claire said. "Anything you wanted." She sneered at me in a way that only a big sister can. "So what did you want to order?"

Boy was she set up, and boy was I going to take advantage of it, because after all, we had twenty fetal pigs coming and she sure didn't get to dissect fetal pigs when she was in sixth grade. And then Danny interrupted.

"And he got to yell at a couple of third graders who got in a fight. He made them sit at table eight and one had to pick up garbage during the whole recess." He leaned back, arms crossed across his chest. Then he stuck his tongue out at Claire.

He may be a pain sometimes, but you can't say that Danny doesn't stick up for his big brother. I made a mental note to remember tomorrow that one of the kids in his class had been picking on him. Maybe it was time for that poor slob to pay a visit to the principal's office, maybe even meet Max.

"So why you?" Dad asked.

"Well, 'cause I'm student council president."

"Yes, and we're very proud of you, but why not one of the teachers?"

Huh. I hadn't thought about that. "I guess they're too busy teaching. And it's just for two days. He'll be back on Monday. Maybe he didn't want to disrupt the classes by bringing in a sub."

He looked at me for a while, spinning a hunk of meat on his fork. I could tell that he wasn't quite sure he approved of this, but didn't really disapprove either. "So did you like it?" he finally asked.

I had to think about that. I missed out on recess with my friends, and got double homework, but overall it was kind of fun. It certainly was different and that was good. I grinned. "I think I did."

"Well, he said, "don't let it go to your head." That was Dad's way of saying you may feel pretty good about yourself today, but don't get too used to it, because sure as we're all sitting around the dinner table, something could knock you on your butt tomorrow. Boy was he right. I just didn't know it yet.

"Remember to be nice to the teachers Billy," my mother said. "They have a hard job."

"And how was ninth grade, Claire?" Dad asked.

Whew. I was off the hot seat. Claire, ever the fount of information, said, "It was okay."

"Anything exciting happen at the high school? Any kids get to be principal there?"

"No," she said, and rolled her eyes. "Can I be excused? I

have lots of homework."

Yeah, you mean texting your friends, but I didn't say anything. I figured I'd save the fetal pigs for sometime that I really needed them. Dad was about to say no, when Mom shook her head at him in that subtle way parents have, and said. "Of course, dear. Clear your dishes first though."

And then there were four at the table. We talked for a while about the field trip that Danny's class is going on to the police department next week. It's a regular third grade field trip. I went on it too when I was in third grade. It was fun, except for the part where they locked us up in jail cells and then pretended that they couldn't find the keys. They said they did that so we'd never do anything bad enough to go to jail. It worked for me. Mom had volunteered to go along as a chaperone with Danny's class, so she wanted to know if there was anything else she needed to know. Suddenly, he slapped his forehead. "I have papers for you but I left them in my desk at school."

"Well, you can bring them home tomorrow. Don't forget," she said. "In fact, Billy, since you're the principal, why don't you stop by Danny's class and remind him to put them in his backpack."

Great. More work for me. Well, I guess I'd have the time. I was finding out that principals really didn't have much to do.

Chapter 19

My Second Day As Principal - Paperwork

The school was only about half a mile from the house, so Danny and I walked to school every morning, and this morning was no different. As we strolled up to the front entrance, I noticed Mr. Johnson's parking place. Everybody knew it was his because it said 'Principal' on the sign right in front of it. Nobody else was allowed to park there, not even Mrs. Madigan or the teachers. It kind of made me wish I had a car. Maybe if I called Grandpa Jake, he'd drive us to school in his golf cart and I could drive through the parking lot and park it in my own special parking space. Except that I was already at school.

We walked through the front door and Danny took off to the left, toward the third-fourth wing. "See ya later," he called as he disappeared around the corner.

"You too." I took off in the opposite direction, toward the sixth grade classes. I knew that I had to check in with Mr. Ward first thing, and then I could go to the office to be principal.

I kind of wandered about a little bit after I left Mr. Ward's class, looking into the primary classes, and making sure that none of the kids were still playing tetherball, or anything on the playground, kind of like Mr. Johnson used to do, so it took me about fifteen minutes to get to the office.

Mrs. Madigan was waiting for me. "Hi, Mrs. Madigan," I said. I walked around the corner and dropped my backpack on the floor in Mr. Johnson's office.

She followed me in. "You need to take care of these right away," she said, and dropped some papers on my desk.

I looked at them. It was a stack about four inches thick. Whoa! What happened? "What's this?"

"Textbook orders for next year," she said. "They're due to the district office by the end of the day. I guess Mr. Johnson forgot about them. Sometimes he doesn't like to finish his paperwork."

Ya think! Four inches of textbook orders! And I have to go through them. Give me some good old fashioned spelling homework any day.

I looked up at her. "What do I need to do?"

"Well, they're all written. You just need to sign them."

Oh, I flashed on the handy signature stamp. I wondered how fast I could stamp four inches of paper.

"Ok," I said. "I can do that." I pulled out Mr. Johnson's chair and started to sit down.

"And make sure that all of the quantities are correct." She

bent over and pulled out two files of papers. "The blue file is the textbook inventory." When I looked up at her, she said, "that's how many books we have now, either in the classrooms or in the book storage room."

The book storage room? I wondered where that was.

"And the red file has the suggested numbers of books for each class, so it's easy. All you have to do is check to make sure that the teachers are getting the right numbers of books. Here, I'll show you." She pulled out one of the order forms. "See, this is Mr. Ward's class. Now if you look at the red file, it says that he needs thirty five math books and reading books and eighteen science books and social studies books."

Thirty-five? Eighteen? Oh yeah. We share books for science and social studies. "Why thirty-five? We only have twenty-nine kids, right?"

"Well, the district says you can have up to thirty-four, and one extra for the teacher makes thirty-five." She pointed further down the list. "And here are the totals for the workbooks and dictionaries."

Then she took out the blue file and pulled Mr. Ward's class inventory from that. "Now you match the blue file inventory with the red file need, and see how many you need to order. See, you have thirty math books in the class now, and one more in the book storage room, so you need to order four." Then she pulled out the order sheet, so I had the blue file, the red file, and the order sheet in front of me. Are you confused yet? I sure was. "It's really pretty simple," she said. "Math textbooks. Need thirty-five, have thirty-one, order four."

It's a good thing I'm pretty good at math. I could tell that I'd be busy. I said, "If the order sheets are already filled in, why do I have to go over them?"

"Oh," she said. "Because these were filled in by the teachers in their last staff meeting, and..." She paused, and then said softly, "Well, I guess I can tell you since you're the principal after all, some of them cheat."

"What do you mean, cheat?"

"Well, they like to have lots of books, so even if they have thirty-five books already, some of them will order another five or ten books, just to have extras, and some of them don't bother to look in the book room, so they don't include the books there." She paused, and then whispered, "I definitely shouldn't say this, but you're going to find out anyway, so here it is. We have a couple of teachers who think this is a waste of their time, so they don't bother to order anything at all, and then Mr. Johnson gets blamed when they don't have books at the beginning of the year."

I stared at her. I had to check to make sure that the teachers did their work right. Something was really wrong with that. I mean, if I didn't get my homework done, I got detention, but I never heard of a teacher getting detention. Then I had a thought. Could I give a teacher detention for filling out the form wrong? Well, could I? After all, I was the principal.

Mrs. Madigan was still talking, so I looked back up at her, but I guess I hadn't missed anything, since she was just showing another example. "Do you understand?" she asked.

I nodded. "Yeah. I need to double check the teachers to

make sure their math was good."

"Well, I wouldn't say that," she started, but then just kinda chuckled, "I guess."

She left and I started working. It was pretty boring, and I found a couple of simple mistakes, where a teacher was off by one or two books, so I corrected them. Then I got to Mrs. McKenzie's class. She had extras of everything, and I mean everything. Take math, for example. According to her inventory, she had thirty-two books in her classroom, and another twelve books in the book storage room, and she was still ordering ten more books. In fact, she was ordering ten more of every book on the order sheet. Something was fishy there. Did she really need fifty-four math books? Or how about the reading book order? According to the inventory sheet, she only had fourteen reading books in the classroom and none in the storage room. But she ordered ten, so she'd still only have twenty-four. I could see what she had done now. She just ordered ten of everything to save time. She didn't pay any attention to what she was supposed to have. As she would have said to me when I was in fourth grade, "If you're not going to take the time to do the job right, you shouldn't bother to do it at all." Well, she sure didn't take the time to do the job right, and I could tell that I'd be working for a while figuring out how to give her detention. You can bet that put a smile on my face.

Textbook orders took all morning. I didn't even get to stop for recess. In fact, I was just stamping the last of them when Mrs. Allistair, the PTA President, came in.

Chapter 20

My Second Day As Principal – The PTA

I had just handed the stack of textbook orders to Mrs. Madigan and she was checking to make sure every one was signed, when Mrs. Allistair came through the front door. I looked over at her. "Hi, Mrs. Allistair. I'll be right with you." She looked kind of puzzled, and then nodded, so I figured her kids told her that I was the principal today.

Mrs. Madigan interrupted me. "Wow, this is really good, Billy. It'll be the first time in years that we've turned in the textbook orders on time."

Huh? I looked at her. "What do you mean?"

"Oh, Mr. Johnson's always at least a week late. He hates checking the teachers' work."

"You mean I didn't have to get them all done today? You mean I could have left them for Mr. Johnson?"

She grinned, kind of like she'd just put something over on me. "Oh, but they are done. Thanks."

I just mumbled a bit under my breath, and then

remembered my leverage with Mrs. Mckenzie. Maybe it was worth it. Then I looked out and saw Mrs. Allistair again. "Hi, come on in."

She came in and sat in the other chair in the office. I sat in Mr. Johnson's chair. She took out a stack of papers and put them on the desk between us. "These are all of the forms for the winter fundraiser. Mr. Johnson already approved them."

"Good," I said. "So what do you want me to do with them?"

"Just leave them for him, I guess. He said that he needed to file them."

"Okay." I'd seen that he had a box marked 'in.' I dropped the forms in there. I couldn't see why she had to come into the office. I was about to find out.

"And we need the multipurpose room all day from January 21st until February 19th."

Uh, sure. I tried to remember a time when the PTA needed the multipurpose room all day, every day, for a month. I must have looked confused, because she said, "Oh, we forgot to talk to Mr. Johnson about that, so he probably didn't tell you."

"No. Why?"

"Why didn't he tell you? I suppose because he didn't know."

"No, why do you need the multipurpose room?"

"For the craft faire."

"Will this be like the craft faire last year?"

"Oh heavens no. Much bigger." She smiled. "I've already signed up lots of people who will be coming here not only to sell their crafts, but to set up booths here so that the kids can participate in making things."

Well, it sounded pretty cool. I could think of a lot of kids who'd really like making crafts. I know that given the choice between grammar and making crafts, I'd choose crafts. Still, I was confused. I remembered going last year. I bought some paper flowers for Mom.

"Didn't the craft faire just last for one day last year? And wasn't it on a Saturday?"

"Well this one will be much bigger."

Then it hit me. She wanted the multipurpose room all day every day for a month? Where were the kids going to eat? And where would Coach Bob be teaching basketball?

"You need the whole multipurpose room?"

"Of course. And if I can get enough artists signed up, we'll take over the library and the computer lab too."

Whoa. The library? The computer lab? I'd be the kid who closed the library and the computer lab? Those were two of the highlights every kid looked forward to every week. You were pretty much guaranteed that you couldn't get homework from either one, so everyone wanted more library and computer, not less.

"I'm not sure we can do that."

"Why not? Any money we earn will go to support activities

at this school. We're hoping to earn three thousand dollars on this event, and that will go toward field trips."

Okay, a lot of money. Then I thought of the textbook orders. They were over twelve thousand dollars. I guess schools took a lot of money to run. So we definitely needed the three thousand dollars.

"But how will the kids go to the library, or the computer lab?"

She looked at me like I was the crazy one and then said, "Oh. They won't."

I frowned. This sounded like a problem. "What about lunch? Where will they eat?"

She smiled at me. Obviously, she had already figured this out. I couldn't wait. "Well, since it's only a month, they can eat outside, or in their classrooms."

Hmm. Every teacher I'd ever had hated having kids in the classroom on rainy day recesses, and that was only fifteen minutes. How would they feel about having them eat lunch in the rooms? I shook my head. If I ever approved something like having kids eating in the classrooms, I'd never get out of sixth grade.

"I don't think the teachers will want the kids eating in the classrooms for a month."

"Well, you're the principal, right?"

"Uh, yeah."

"So that means you're the boss. Tell them they have to. After all, we're making money for field trips. Besides, they can always eat outside."

"What if it rains?" I asked.

"What if it doesn't?"

"It rains a lot in January."

She was insistent. "But maybe it won't."

Hmm. This wasn't going anywhere. I guess it was time for me to make a Principal decision. "Mrs. Allistair," I said. "You can't have the multipurpose room for a month, or the computer lab, or the library."

She just stared at me for a minute, kind of like she was waiting for me to back down and say that maybe she'd heard me wrong and I really did think it was a good idea for her to take over the multipurpose room and the computer lab and the library for a month because raising money for field trips was more important than kids having a place to eat. When she continued to stare, I said, "I'm sorry, but you just can't."

"Well!" she said, but it really sounded like she was blowing the word out at me, "Whelllll! We'll see about that. Mr. Johnson has never treated me so rudely. I will be sure to talk to him when he returns about your attitude, and you can forget about field trip money for your class." Then she sneered at me. "I think we should cut off Danny's class too."

Then she got up, and stomped out of the room and slammed the door. I was impressed. I only wished that Claire could have been there. She did a much better job of stomping out of a room and slamming a door than Claire ever had. Maybe it was because she was older and had more practice.

Then I leaned back in my chair. My heart was racing and I needed a minute to calm down. I guess I'd have to tell Mr. Johnson that my meeting with Mrs. Allistair hadn't gone very well. I looked up at the clock. It was almost time for lunch.

Chapter 21

My Second Day As Principal - Lunch

I've decided that I really like the little kids. I mean, they're loud, and their voices are kind of screechy, but every group wanted me to sit at their table. I sat with first graders this time, and we talked about being a principal a little, but mostly about what their dogs and cats like to do, and boogers. I don't know why, I didn't start the conversation. They were a lot nicer than Mrs. Allistair. And when eating time was over, nobody stomped their feet or slammed the door.

And then the older kids came in for lunch. Looking back now, I should have known that something was just a little off. I don't know what, I guess there was just something in the air, some tension or something. I don't know.

It took them about ten minutes to go through the food line, and I was able to meet with Paul and the guys while they got their stuff and sat down. Then the lunch lady chased them back to their tables, and I started to wander around, just like the day before, just like Mr. Johnson did.

This time, I went to one of the fourth grade classes. I'd stopped by this classroom before I went to the office in the morning, and talked with the kid who'd been bugging Danny, so now I just wanted to make sure he hadn't forgotten what would happen if he didn't leave Danny alone. You have to check those things. Sometimes kids do forget. Like with Michael the day before, I just wanted to make sure that he hadn't been so focused on playing soccer that he didn't hear me. Anyway, the kid saw me coming and said, "Hi Billy." I said hi and asked if there had been any trouble between him and Danny. He shook his head. Good. He remembered.

Then I went to the fifth graders. I wanted to talk to Max, just to make sure again that we were going to work on fractions after school. Sometimes he forgets too. Also, I wanted the other kids to see that Max was a friend of mine. I figured I could keep using that.

That's when I heard a loud, "Hey!"

Everyone's head spun around. Mine did too. One of the kids in the other sixth grade was standing up, yelling at another kid. I stared at him. His hair looked funny. Then I could tell what it was. He was covered with the day's special, spaghetti. While I watched, he peeled a handful of spaghetti off of his head and threw it at one of the other kids down the table. The kid ducked and it hit the girl next to him. Everybody got real quiet then. I knew her. She was kind of prissy and didn't like to get dirty. She even hated soccer at PE. But today, I guess she didn't care, because she took her yogurt and threw it at spaghetti head, who ducked. Unfortunately, one of the lunch ladies was right behind him and she got thoroughly splattered with pink yogurt. Her eyes went wide, and I thought she was going to grab somebody by the neck. And all this happened before I even had a chance to blink. Seconds. Nanoseconds!

I yelled and tried to get over there, because I figured that's what the principal should do, but there was a table of fifth graders in the way, so I had to run around them. By the time I got to the sixth grade table, there was food flying everywhere, and I don't just mean everywhere at the sixth grade table. It seemed like every kid in the multipurpose room was throwing spaghetti and yogurt and burritos and taco salads. It was a gross, disgusting mess.

Then I heard the whistle. It was main lunch lady, the one who was usually behind the counter. She was strict, and mean, and serious, and she blew that whistle, and then blew it again, and then blew it again.

The room got really quiet as she walked out from behind her counter. She was slow, like a leopard sneaking up on its prey, and every kid in that room must have felt like a wounded antelope at that moment. She had her whistle in one hand and discipline tickets in the other, and you could tell that she meant business.

She was half way to the sixth grade table and the boys who had started it all, when a plate full of spaghetti came twirling through the air and caught her full in the face. It was a horrible, disgusting sight. This was not a pretty lady to begin with, and having a plate full of spaghetti all over her face didn't improve her looks at all.

I stared, and then remembering that I was supposed to be the principal, I yelled as loud as I could, "Stop it now!"

That was just before I got pelted with yogurt, and peas, and salsa from the taco salad.

Some kid yelled "Food Fight!" And all I could do was back away, out of the field of fire.

It took a good fifteen minutes to get the place settled down. By then, every kid and every adult in the room was covered in a messy mash of lunch. The walls were a mess, and even Joe, our custodian who's seen more than his share of disgusting messes, had to admit that this was the biggest food disaster in the history of the school, maybe in the history of all schools.

So what could I do? There was only one of me, and over two hundred of the other kids. I looked around. The lunch ladies were furious, and mostly with me for not stopping the food fight. Hey, did they even bother to look at me? I was busy ducking for my life and I still got covered with a gooey mess.

We locked the doors for the rest of lunch, and made the kids start cleaning up, but they didn't do much. The ones who started the fight just laughed and refused, and one said, "I ain't cleanin' and there's nothin' you can do about it."

And he was pretty much right. I mean, I guess I could suspend him, but the multipurpose room would still be trashed, and all the kids knew that his parents both worked, so he'd just get a three-day weekend. He liked being suspended.

In the end, I made him and the other kids who started the food fight stay at their tables for the rest of the day, even if they didn't help clean up.

A bunch of the kids ended up going to the office so that they could call home and have their mothers bring them clean clothes. And whom do you think those mothers were mad at? That's right, me. How can that possibly be fair? I mean, there I was, innocently helping out with lunch, when a bunch of hooligans start a food fight, and I get blasted with a gross mess, and then I get blamed. I repeat, how can that possibly be fair?

So I was feeling pretty low, not to mention sticky, when Mrs. Madigan said, "Don't feel too bad. Mr. Johnson will be back on Monday."

That just made me feel worse. I'd let everybody down. I was a failure.

I had two meetings with parents that afternoon. Their kids were both in first grade, so they didn't know about the great food fight. They just kept looking at me throughout the meetings and I could tell that they wondered what had happened to my hair and my shirt. And then neither meeting went the way that they wanted, so they were both mad at me too, and promised to tell Mr. Johnson when he got back what a lousy job I was doing.

I didn't think I could feel any worse when I finally got up to leave at three. I still had to meet with Max and go over fractions. On the way out, I looked into the multipurpose room. There was Joe, on his hands and knees, using a knife of some sort to scrape food off of the floor. He looked up at me, and we made eye contact, and in that moment, somehow I could tell that he blamed me too.

I skipped the tutoring session with Max. I just went straight home and locked myself in my room. I didn't even come out for dinner.

Chapter 22

Dinner with Claire

Claire knocked on the door at about eight.

"Who's there?" I called.

"It's your sister. Can I come in?" She usually would have just come in, but she doesn't want me to walk in on her without knocking, so I guess this was her way of saying the rules applied both ways.

"Sure." I sat on the edge of the bed and wiped my eyes. I hadn't really been crying, but just in case... She walked through the door and closed it behind her. I noticed that she had a plate wrapped in foil. "Dinner?" I asked.

She nodded and sat cross-legged on the floor, the plate and a glass of milk in front of her. As she took off the foil, steam started to rise from the plate and the aromas wafted in my direction. Suddenly, I was famished. I popped down across from her and checked out the plate. Barbecued chicken, broccoli, part of a baked potato, and some salad. I reached for a chicken leg and started chewing meat off the end. It was delicious, one of my favorites. Then I looked across at her. She could be a real pain sometimes, like the night before at dinner, but she always seemed to know when somebody was hurting, and just what to do to help. "Thanks," I said.

She let me eat for a while before saying, "So what happened?"

"What did Danny say?"

She just shook her head. "He wouldn't tell us anything. I guess he was protecting you."

Hmm. Just when you thought you had the kid all figured out. Using my fork, I carved a hunk off the baked potato and popped it into my mouth. She was still staring at me, so I just shrugged. "Everything went wrong and it's all my fault."

"I doubt that everything went wrong. And I'm sure it wasn't all your fault. What happened?"

Somehow, getting some chicken and potato into my belly made things seem a little better. I looked down at the broccoli. Naw. Why take chances. I was feeling better with the chicken. Broccoli might just ruin that. The first chicken leg was just about sucked clean, so I picked up the other one and started in on that. "Everybody's mad at me."

"Everybody? Really? I'm not. Danny's not. Who exactly?" she asked.

"The kids, the parents, the teachers, even Joe, our custodian.

"Why are they mad?"

I put down the chicken leg and sighed deeply. I might as well just tell her. She'd find out soon enough anyway. "Okay." I started to recount the day, starting with the food fight. I told her about the kid who started it all by throwing a plate full of spaghetti, and how I got hit with yogurt, and everything else, and even how the lunch lady looked with the spaghetti dangling out of her hair. By then, Clair was grinning, and I couldn't help myself. I grinned too. It was kind of funny, especially the lunch lady. Then I remembered that I was supposed to be the principal, the one in charge, and food fights weren't really allowed. "So there was this huge mess, and I made everyone stay in and start cleaning up during recess, so all the food ladies were mad because there was a big food fight, and the kids were mad because they didn't get recess, and Joe was still cleaning goop off of the floor when I left."

Claire was quiet for a long time. Finally, she said, "Do you suppose that's the first time there's ever been a food fight in the multipurpose room?"

I hadn't thought about that. I couldn't remember another time. I grimaced. "Probably."

She shook her head. "I can remember a couple of times when I was at school there. One time, kids were even throwing burritos up against the ceiling to see if they could get them to stick."

I tried to imagine that. "Really?"

Then she laughed. "Really. I remember that part of a burrito fell down the next day on Mr. Johnson. He really couldn't do anything, since he'd already suspended the kids who threw it up to the ceiling and they weren't even at school, so he just yelled at everybody, and we had to try not to laugh at the spot of taco sauce that he missed on his head."

I had to laugh at that too. Then I remembered that everyone was still mad at me. "But I was in charge. It was my fault."

"Come on," she said. "Did you throw any food?"

I shook my head vigorously. "No, I kept trying to get the kids to stop."

"So they got out of control. That wasn't your fault, it was theirs." She hesitated for a minute, and then said something that made a lot of sense. "Do you think any of those kids are allowed to have food fights at home?"

Thinking about it that way, yeah, the kids were way out of line, and everyone who had to stay and clean up deserved it. Well, except for the kids who just tried to get out of the way, but still, they didn't do anything to try and stop the ones who were throwing food. At least I tried to do that. I started to shake my head. "No. Mom and Dad'd kill us if we ever had a food fight at dinner. I guess the other parents would be pretty much the same."

"So it wasn't really your fault," she said. "The kids who threw food were to blame, and so were the lunch ladies. What do you think happens when Mr. Johnson has a lunchtime meeting away from the school? Is there a food fight every time? No. The lunch ladies handle it themselves. This time, they didn't. Kids who throw food at lunch will throw food whether you're there or not."

I looked at my sister with a new sense of respect. Maybe she learned this kind of stuff in high school. I never thought about it before. Maybe Joe would forget he was mad at me by Monday. Maybe. It probably depended upon whether there was still food smeared all over the walls.

Chapter 23

Problems With Monkeys

So there I was, eating dinner, and thinking that maybe the food fight wasn't really my fault, and maybe I shouldn't feel so bad. Then I thought about Mrs. Allistair and the other parents. My bad day hadn't ended with the food fight. "And the parents are mad at me too."

"All of the parents? Or just some?" she asked.

"Well, Mrs. Allistair, our PTA president is so mad she said she'd tell Mr. Johnson I was doing a bad job as principal."

"Why's she mad?"

So I told her all about how the PTA wanted to run a craft faire to raise money for field trips, and they planned to close the multipurpose room and maybe the library and computer lab for a month in January and February and I said no.

"You're kidding me, right?"

"No, I really did say no, and she's really steamed but I

figured that if I closed the multipurpose room and the computer lab and the library, then the kids and teachers would be mad. I wasn't sure what to do, so I said no and told her she'd have to talk to Mr. Johnson."

"Seems reasonable."

"But she'd already signed up a bunch of people to work in the craft faire, and didn't want to have to tell them it was all off."

Claire nodded for a moment, and then gave me a funny look, "There's an interesting line I learned the other day in my social studies class."

Great, I thought. Now I was getting interesting lines from my sister when everyone in the school was mad at me. Oh well, I had nothing better to do. "Ok. I'm listening. What's your line?"

"When you have a problem, they say you have a monkey on your back."

Huh? How could that make any sense? I was curious though. "Why?"

"Well, I guess a long time ago, even before Uncle Albert was born, people sometimes had monkeys on their backs."

Now I was really confused. How did they get monkeys on their backs? I mean, I rode my bike all over town, and I had never once had to watch out for falling monkeys just hoping to hop onto my back. "That doesn't even make any sense."

"I guess if you live in India, or Africa, or someplace like that it's a problem."

"You mean people just have monkeys following them around and jumping onto their backs?"

She shrugged. "I guess, and from what my teacher said, it's really hard to get them off."

Well at least that part made sense, not that I had any experience with monkeys grabbing on, but they could probably hold on pretty tight, and the ones I saw in the zoo looked like they had pretty sharp teeth, and I suppose they had claws too. Still, it might be kind of fun having a spider monkey on my back. Can you imagine going to school with a monkey instead of a backpack? Maybe that's what I needed on Monday. People would be so happy to see the monkey, they'd forget they were mad at me. But my sister was still talking. I'd missed most of it.

"...problem is like a monkey on your back," she said. I just stared at her and she sighed. "Are you even listening?"

"Uh..."

"I said, according to my teacher, if you have a problem, it's kind of like having a monkey on your back. It's hard to get rid of."

I thought about that for a while. Problems equal monkeys on your back equal problems. Well, I guess that if you had a monkey on your back and it didn't want to get off that might be kind of a problem. Ok, it sort of made sense.

"Anyway, it's just a line, an idiom. When you have a problem, you have a monkey on your back."

Ah, an idiom. We'd studied them in school. Something you say, that doesn't make any sense, because it means something entirely different from what it really sounds like.

I remember my fifth grade teacher taught us several idioms. One was 'burr under his skin.' It meant get mad, because if you had a burr under your skin, you'd be mad about it because it would hurt, and then Paul's dad told him it was really 'burr up his butt,' which I guess would really hurt, and make you even madder, but they can't say butt in school. I looked at my sister with new respect. A monkey on your back. That meant you had a problem. Interesting. But, there was something missing. "So what's that got to do with anything?"

"Well, Mr. Albertson said that everyone has a monkey on his back sometimes, and they always try to give their monkey to somebody else."

Ok. Quick translation. Everybody has problems and they try to give those problems to somebody else. I nodded at her. It made sense. Like the time I got in trouble for putting Danny's bike in the tree. Remember that? He was being a pest, which caused me and my friends a problem, so we put his bike in the tree, which transferred the problem to him. But then we got in trouble and had to get the bike down out of the tree, which transferred the problem back to us. Hmmm. According to my sister, that monkey was moving all over the place. "You sure that works?"

"Well, look at it this way. Mrs. Allistair had already promised the craft people that they could have the multipurpose room for a month, and maybe even the computer lab and the library, right?"

"Yeah."

"So that was the monkey on her back. It was a problem because she didn't talk with Mr. Johnson first to make sure he'd allow it."

I wasn't sure where this was going, but it was a nice distraction. I just nodded. "Ok."

"So then she talked to you. She wanted you to let her have the rooms for a month, and she didn't care if that caused a problem for you with the teachers or the kids. She just wanted to get rid of her problem with the craft people, right?"

She was looking at me, and suddenly I got it. Finding a place to put the craft people was her monkey. If she couldn't do it, they'd be mad at her. So she told me that she needed the rooms, which meant it would turn into my monkey because I'd have people mad at me but the craft people would think she was pretty good. I grinned. "So she was trying to give me her monkey."

Claire picked up a piece of broccoli and popped it into her mouth. She was like that, anything on your plate was always fair game. Hey, 'fair game,' there's another idiom. Well, at least she was eating the broccoli. There was a little chicken left, but she had enough sense not to try and snatch that. "Mr. Albertson says that everybody goes through life with a group of monkeys on their back, and they're always trying to give them to somebody else. And everybody else is trying to avoid taking the monkeys because they already have their own."

Huh. That just made way too much sense. Usually having an older sister was kind of like having chicken pox, but somehow she'd gotten pretty smart. It must be high school. Then I thought about the other parents who were mad at me. They had their monkeys too. I said, "You know, some of the parents were mad at me today because their kids were messing around in class, and not doing their work, and so their teachers were upset. And when they met with me, I just said that they needed to get their kids to work in class instead of playing around." Claire grinned at me and I said what she was about to say. "They were trying to pass off their monkeys, and I just threw them back. No wonder they were mad." I picked up the last of the chicken and nibbled at it.

Claire said, "That's right. So it wasn't really all your fault, just monkeys."

I nodded. "Yeah. Huh." I looked across at her and said, "You know what Mr. Johnson needs in his office?" When she looked at me, she seemed confused, so I said, "He needs a sign that says, 'No Monkeys Needed Here.'"

She giggled then, and said, "And it should have a picture of him with a monkey on his back." Then she turned serious. "You know though, some things are your fault, and you can't blame anybody else," she said.

I looked at her. Uh oh. What was coming now? "What?"

"Well, your hair is disgusting. And I think that yogurt is starting to spoil. You need a shower!"

We both started to laugh then, and I looked down at my shirt. It was still decorated with spaghetti sauce. I pulled it off and tossed it at her, and she batted it back. Just then, I saw Mom peek in. When she saw us laughing, she smiled and backed out.

Chapter 24

Retired

So I was officially retired as the principal of W. H. Carpenter Elementary School. And I have to tell you, it felt really good. I'd be able to go back to school on Monday and just be a sixth grader. Nobody would be mad at me because the multipurpose room was messed up, or because their kid was fooling around in class and they were looking for someone else to blame for his bad grades, or for not letting them use the multipurpose room for a month. I could have walked on air. Those monkeys were officially gone.

Paul called Saturday morning. He and a bunch of the other guys were getting up a game of basketball at the park after lunch and he wanted to know if I was interested. Can you imagine me saying no? I didn't think so. Of course I was interested.

I rode my bike over there and was one of the first to arrive. We just fooled around for a while, playing HORSE, while we waited for the others, and can you guess what the conversation was about? Of course you can. 'What's it like being the principal?'

So I told them. "At first, it was pretty cool. I got to sign some orders, and that means that sixth grade gets to dissect fetal pigs this year." I couldn't really tell them much more after that, because everybody wanted to know what a fetal pig was. Yeah, it'd be gross, but it was going to be pretty interesting too.

So then I told them about eating with first and second graders, and talking about boogers and stuff, and playing basketball with the fourth graders, and all the other good stuff. Then I mentioned Mrs. Allistair. I told them that she wanted to take the multipurpose room for a whole month in the middle of winter. They figured that out right away. "Where would we eat?" Mark asked.

"She figured we could eat outside or in classrooms." He just looked at me like I was from Mars or something, so I said, "Yeah, that's what I thought too, so I said no, and now she's really mad at me."

"Wow," Jose said. "Mad just because she couldn't close the multipurpose room when it's raining outside?"

"Yeah, and she wanted to close the library and the computer lab too." Now they really stared, so I said, "It gets worse. After her, there were the parents who thought that it was my fault that their kids were getting bad grades when they kept acting up in class and never did any work."

Paul had arrived by then, and he wanted to know where he could get parents like that. "Shoot," he said, "I remember trying to get away with stuff when I was in third grade and my parents met with the teacher and they all yelled at me. It was like a tag team wrestling match. I hardly knew where to look to see who was going to be shouting at me next, and then when I got home, I got grounded for a month and had to make up all the work I'd missed."

"Exactly! When I got in trouble with Mrs. McKenzie for calling her homework detention stupid, it was even worse when I got home, but these parents seemed to think that it would be my fault if their kid didn't get his way."

Then I mentioned how many mothers were mad at me because their kids got their clothes dirty in the food fight, and the guys just kind of lowered their heads and shuffled their feet. Yeah. They were there, and a couple of them threw spaghetti and burritos and stuff. Paul said, "Sorry about that. I don't know what happened. It was fun for a while, but after it was all over, it seemed kind of dumb."

"Yeah, me too," said Mark.

The others agreed, and it got quiet until I said, "Hey, we're here to play basketball, and I'm retired as principal, so let's go have fun." So we chose up teams, and I got to be one of the captains. I'm not that good at basketball, so I never get to be captain, but I guess it was the guys' way of saying they were sorry for the food fight.

We played to thirty, and my team won 30 to 28. It was close.

Chapter 25

Monday Morning

One of the best walks I ever took to Carpenter School was on Monday morning. Danny and I got to the school just before eight o'clock, and walked in the front door. Then he went his way and I went mine. And I didn't have to think about checking in with Mr. Ward and then going back to the office. It was just going to be school all day. Reading, Language, Math, Science, and PE, with a lot of recess mixed in. What a relief.

When I got in line outside the classroom, a lot more kids wanted to know what it was like being principal. I told them some, and it seemed that just about everybody was sorry about me getting in trouble over the food fight. I mean, they probably would have thought it was fair if I'd thrown food, but since I was just trying to stop everyone else, it really wasn't. Of course, Ryan wasn't sorry, but since he was one of the ones who started it and then refused to help clean up, I really didn't expect him to have a sudden change of heart. He'd probably be happy if there was another food fight at lunch today and since I made him stay in during recess, I figured I should stay away from him for a while.

 Mr. Ward opened the door and let everybody in. When I passed him, he said, "Welcome back," and the way he was smiling, I could tell that he really meant it. It kind of made me feel good all over.

He took roll while we were getting our stuff out and doing the math worksheet on our desks, and then called my name, "Billy, you want to take this roll sheet up to the office? You know your way there, right?"

He was grinning, and a lot of the kids snickered, but I just said, "Sure." I took the sheet, and said, "Be right back." Then I walked down the hallway to the office.

On the way, I passed a couple of first graders walking hand in hand with their roll sheet. One of them pointed at me and said, "There's the principal."

"Not any more," I said. They looked really confused, so I told them that Mr. Johnson was back, and I got to go back to being a normal sixth grader.

But they still didn't get it, and one of them pointed at me and started chanting, "You're the principal, you're the principal," so I just waved and ran on to the office.

And found out he was right. Mrs. Madigan was waiting for me. I handed her the roll sheet and started to turn around when she said, "Don't go yet."

Huh? Now what? She handed me a piece of paper. It looked like she'd printed out an email, so I looked at the top. It was from Elmer Johnson, whoever that was. I read it. And began to feel sick. You might as well see the whole thing.

Mrs. Madigan,

You wouldn't believe what happened here. They decided that my act is one of the best they've ever seen and want me to perform on America's Most Amezing Acts. How about that for exciting!

We'll spend this whole week practicing, and they plan to set me up with a professional band and acrobats to help me to polish my performance. Thursday, they film for the show and Friday they'll review the film to make sure everything is ready and doesn't need to be redone.

Tell Billy I'm really glad he's working as principal while I'm gone, because I know he's doing a great job. I'll see you next Monday.

Elmer

I couldn't believe it. Just when I thought I'd be able to go back to being a kid, I was going to be stuck with a whole week of principal stuff.

"You might as well go pick up your backpack," she said. "I'll call Mr. Ward."

I looked down at the email and read it again. You'd think a real principal would at least be able to spell the name of the TV show he was going to be in. And then I turned around and trudged back to my class. I passed the first graders on my way. I asked what had taken them so long to get to the office, and one held out his hand to show me a beetle. "I caught him by the drinking fountain. You want to pet him?" I shook my head and said no, so they waved and ran into the office, "Goodbye, Principal!"

Chapter 26

Reinforcements

Mr. Ward wasn't happy to see me going back to the office. I guess he thought that sixth graders should be going to sixth grade. I kind of wanted to agree. As I was about to go out the door, he said, "Stop by after school. I'll have your homework ready for you."

"Gee thanks, you're a real prince," I thought. But I didn't say anything. I just nodded and put on my pack and walked back to the office. The two first graders were playing with the beetle under the drinking fountain. Since I was the principal again, I took each one by the hand and walked them back to their classroom. On the way, I found out that one had a sister who was in really big trouble because she decided to get her nose pierced and didn't tell their Mom until she asked why she was wearing a bandage.

So I found myself back in the office. Fortunately, it was a quiet morning, and since Mr. Ward had already started the math lesson when I was in the classroom, I knew what pages we were working on, so I figured I might as well do my homework. The assignment wasn't on the board yet, but he usually assigned either the odd problems or the even ones on the page. Just to be safe, I did them all.

I finished a little before recess. It was quiet, so I went out to play. I mean, I was the principal, right? So if I wanted to get in a game of soccer during recess, nobody could stop me. When we finished the game, I talked with the guys about a plan I was thinking of.

I was walking back to class when Maddy Fisher came running up. "Hey," she said.

"Hey. What's up Maddy?"

"I hear you're principal for another week. Are we still having our meeting today?"

Meeting? I was confused for just a second, and then I remembered that Maddy was the secretary of the student council. "Is that today? Didn't Mrs. Kinney send out a reminder?"

"You were supposed to give it to her last Thursday, remember?"

I was. I forgot. I could see that this principal thing was getting in the way of lots of other stuff. "Uh, I'll send the notices out this morning. Since I'm not going to be in class, I should be able to deliver them myself."

"Good," she said. "I'll tell Mrs. Kinney." Then she ran off to her class line. I could see that Mrs. Kinney was already waiting for her. I just waved and then turned toward the office.

Where Mrs. Allistair was waiting for me. Great. Another chance to get chewed on. She started to talk as soon as I walked through the door, and followed me into Mr. Johnson's office, but I ignored her until I'd written a reminder to write and deliver the student council notes. I usually gave them to Mrs. Kinney and she put them in teachers' boxes, but I knew who was supposed to get them.

Finally, I turned around. Mrs. Allistair was still talking, but since I hadn't been paying any attention, I had no idea what it was about. "and so I told them we couldn't."

Uh, couldn't what? "I'm sorry," I said, "but I had something else I needed to remember so that's what I wrote down. I wasn't really listening."

"Well I never met such a rude boy!" she blurted. Then she stared at me as if she wanted something, but I'd already told her I was sorry for not listening, so I just stared back. Finally, she said, "I was talking about the craft faire."

"Oh. Anything new?"

"Well I expected to see Mr. Johnson here, but I can see that he's not back yet."

"Next Monday," I said.

"I wanted to tell him that since we can't hold the craft faire in the multipurpose room like we wanted, we won't be able to raise nearly as much money, so we can't give the money to the school for field trips." She folded her arms across her chest and just stared at me, kind of like I should wilt and beg her to please reconsider.

But I didn't. "Well, I guess you'll just have to wait until Monday to see Mr. Johnson."

"So you don't want kids to take field trips? You don't think that's important? You don't like field trips?"

I thought for a minute before answering. Hmm. In the first place, I couldn't ever remember not having to collect money for field trips from my parents. Even if it was just a dollar or two, I always had to get something. Parents usually drove, so I guess it was for admission to a museum or something. I always gave it to my teacher and she decided how to use it. So I wasn't sure which field trips we wouldn't be able to go on if the PTA didn't have a craft faire. Maybe they'd pay for extra trips, or maybe some kids can't get their parents to pay. I didn't know.

But I did know one thing. Even though all the kids liked eating outside on special days in the fall and the spring, nobody wanted to eat outside when it was raining. And nobody and certainly no teacher, wanted to eat in the classroom every day for a month.

"I really like field trips," I told her, "so whatever Mr. Johnson decides is fine with me. I'll bet he's smart enough to find a solution I just can't think of."

That seemed to help a little, and she never really figured out that what I really meant was that maybe he'd find a solution that she wasn't smart enough to think of.

"Harrumph," she said, and then she just turned around and left. And she called me rude? I guess when kids do something you don't like, it's rude. When adults do the same thing to kids, it's okay.

I hand delivered each of the student council

announcements before lunch. Some of the kids were surprised, but everybody promised to be there. We'd be meeting at lunch time in the library, so the notice didn't just tell them about the meeting, it had a part that gave them permission to get out about five minutes early so that they could go through the lunch line first.

By then, it was almost lunchtime. I walked over to the multipurpose room. The lunch ladies were there, setting up the tables. I looked around but couldn't see any evidence of the food fight on Friday. Well, not too much. Some of the paper on the walls where the kids displayed art work was a little stained, but the kids' work had already been taken down since it was the end of the month, and the teachers usually put up new paper when the new work went up. The floor was clean, and the tables and the benches were all clean, and even the ball bin, where somebody had landed a whole plate of spaghetti, looked like it had been washed out. Wow. Joe had really done a job. He was helping to set up tables, so I went over and told him how good it looked.

"Yeah," he said. "Bunch of kids came in after school and helped to clean up."

Hmm. I didn't know that. I guess I'd been in such a hurry to get away that I was gone by the time they showed up.

I was going to ask who they were, when the first graders started to come through the line, so I went over to help. The fifth and sixth grade classes take turns sending a couple of kids to help with lunch, but I've done that job, and it's never enough, so I knew that first graders needed help at the beginning of the year finding their lunch cards, and finding their tables even though the cards are all organized alphabetically on the rack and they sit at the same table every day. Even though you tell them every day, it takes a while for them to figure it out.

While I worked, I had a chance to talk with the main lunch lady. You remember her? The one who got hit in the face with a full plate of spaghetti? I told her I was sorry about that, but she just said that I didn't throw the plate, so it wasn't my fault. Then she laughed about it. I couldn't believe it. Here was an old lady who got hit in the face with a plate full of spaghetti, and she was laughing. She said she wanted to join in and throw it back, but figured she'd get in trouble and might lose her job. That's crazy! Can you imagine what would have happened if the lunch ladies had started throwing food too? I started to laugh then, because if they'd been throwing food, then maybe the teachers would have come in and joined in too, and I'd seen Mr. Ward throwing a football to the boys in the class. He was a pitcher on his college baseball team and could probably throw a yogurt all the way across the playground. Talk about a mess!

I ended up eating with a different first grade class, and we didn't talk about boogers this time. They'd heard about the food fight, and wanted all the details. I thought their eyes might pop right out of their heads when I told them about the lunch lady getting hit in the face with the plate of spaghetti, and they wanted to know if some of the kids got in trouble. I told them that they had to stay in and clean up and didn't get to go out and play. Then I told them that lots of their moms were really angry too, about them getting food on their clothes, and that launched us into a whole conversation about table manners at dinnertime. Funny, nobody had rules for throwing food at home, just rules for not throwing it. In fact, the closest we got to food fights at home was one girl who said that her brother threw his peas at her once, and he got sent straight to his room and didn't get any more dinner or dessert. I didn't mention that the lunch ladies wished they'd been able to join in on the food fight.

After the little kids left, I talked to the lunch ladies about my plan. You remember, I mentioned that I'd talked with the guys after soccer? Naw. You probably forgot, but I did. Anyway, I told them that my sixth grade friends had volunteered to split up and sit with the younger kids and make sure that nobody threw any food today. I'm not sure that they thought it was a good idea, but hey, I was the principal, so I got to make the rules.

I may not like getting yelled at, but making the rules is cool.

Then I got surprised. Paul talked to the class after recess, and they came up with an even better plan. You see, I was going to have one sixth grader sit at each table, but when they came in, the whole class was split into groups of boys and girls, and each group sat at one of the other tables so that they could talk with the other kids and make sure that they knew just how embarrassed everyone was about making a mess.

I visited each of the tables. And at every table, somebody said they were sorry about the food fight. I was sure proud of my class. In fact, lunch went so smoothly that I squeezed in next to some fourth graders and finished my lunch with them. In fact, since they were just eating and not fooling around, everybody was able to get out to play about five minutes early.

On my way outside, I saw Max. Remember Max? I was

supposed to tutor him on fractions, but then I just went home, so I figured I had to tell him I was sorry too. So I ran over to him. "Max," I called just before he went out the door.

He looked over at me and then we both spoke at once. "Uh, sorry about Friday."

It turned out that he wasn't even home after school on Friday, so I couldn't have tutored him anyway. And you'll never believe where he was. I couldn't believe where he was. This might be another thing to guess at and write in the back of the book, but no peeking first.

Okay, did you write it down? Good. Here's the story. I'll bet you guessed wrong.

Max was the one who grabbed a bunch of other guys and helped Joe to clean up the multipurpose room! Just when you think you've got somebody figured out, they go and do something like that.

That afternoon, I met with a mom with a kindergartener who was getting bugged by another kid, so I told her I'd check it out, and wrote another reminder note for myself. Then she thanked me for working so hard as the student principal. So all in all, it was a pretty good day.

Chapter 27

That Night

At dinner that night, Danny told everyone that I was principal again. Dad seemed upset. "Aren't you supposed to be going to school? You're not really supposed to be running it, are you? What does Mr. Ward think about this?"

I just shrugged my shoulders. "I guess it's okay with him. He seems a little upset, but he hasn't told me I can't leave. And he's sure been giving me plenty of homework."

He grunted. "Describe plenty of homework."

"Well, today I did twice as much math as everybody else, and I have some spelling homework, and some reading." I paused as he digested that, and then added, "And they're working on writing a letter to convince somebody to do something in class, so he added that too."

"That it?"

I shook my head. "Naw. Today was science day, so I have some stuff to read and questions to answer, and a book report due Friday."

That seemed to please him. "All right. So long as you're still getting your sixth grade work done." He stuck a fork full of broccoli in his mouth and chewed for a moment. "What are you planning to write about?"

"The book report?"

"The letter."

"Oh, well according to Mrs. Madigan, I have to write something for the monthly newsletter anyway, so I was going to write something to parents telling them that when their kids mess up in class, they should tell the kids to pay attention and do their work instead of blaming it on the teacher."

He looked surprised, but he was smiling, so I could tell he approved. I cut off a bite of chicken, and was about to put it in my mouth when he said, "Do parents really blame the teacher?"

I told him about the ones I'd talked to who seemed to think it was the teacher's fault that their kids were getting bad grades when they spent their time talking to their friends and running around the classroom instead of working. "Some of them even blamed me," I said. "I thought that was pretty unfair."

Then he grinned and winked at my mother. "Guess we did a pretty good job of making sure these kids follow the rules in school."

That got Claire going. "Ya think?" She started waving her fork around, even though it had a big hunk of chicken on it. "I still remember when I was in second grade and Mrs.

Allen called you because I forgot to turn in my homework. I had to do it over even though I'd already done it." She looked around at us, eyes wide, and added, "and then in seventh grade Mr. Willert told you at the parent teacher conference that I was talking too much in class. I got grounded for a week. We can't get away with anything!"

That got Danny going, and I had to add my own stories. And by the time we got done with that line of talk, dinner was over and Mom was dishing up strawberries for dessert. Dad wasn't quite done though. "You want help with that letter?"

Hmm. No matter how good my letter was, he'd make me re-write it. So I was about to say no, but then I figured that since it was going in the school newsletter, it might not be a bad idea to have him look at it. Still, I didn't really want to have to write it twice. No way to win. "Sure."

He smiled and then said, "I see that the circus is going to be at the arena next month. I can't remember the last time they came through, but you guys were too young. So I thought maybe it would make a good family outing." He looked at Mom. "What do you think?"

A circus? Are you kidding me? I've heard of them. I guess they have elephants and lions and acrobats and clowns and shoot guys out of a canon and stuff, but I've never been to one. I looked at my mother.

She just smiled. "That'd be fun. When? I'll put it on the calendar."

Only Claire scowled, but she knew better than to try to complain about an official family outing, even if she had gotten way too cool to be seen with her little brothers in

129

public. Then I looked over at Danny. He was making a monster out of his strawberries and whipped cream. I'd talk to Claire. Maybe we could figure out a way to leave him at home.

I'd finished my dessert, so I asked for permission to be excused, and started to stand when Mom said, "Isn't it your night to wash the dishes?"

I wanted to scream. I'd been principal all day, and had double homework, and all the parents who wanted to meet with me after school. Plus today I had to write the agenda for the Student Council meeting. You'd think somebody might have some mercy on me, but nooooooo. I still had to do the dishes. I looked at Danny. He was still playing with his strawberries. Claire was trying to look at her phone for a text without being discovered under the table, so there was no help there. I stood up. "I guess," I said.

I started to gather up the dinner dishes when Dad stood too. "I'll help," he said. "We can talk about your letter."

Dad? Help with dishes? This was new. I hadn't seen him helping with dishes since Claire and I had been old enough to wash them without breaking too many. Of course, he wanted to talk about the letter, which probably meant more writing.

"Oh, I forgot to mention," Mom said as I carried the first load out to the kitchen. "I got a letter from Great Aunt Beattie." She looked over at my brother who looked up from his monster just long enough to shrug. "Danny, you were supposed to remind me." That was one of Danny's jobs now that he was in third grade. He was the new mailman, opening the mail while Mom made dinner, and writing letters. But you probably don't care too much about that. Then Mom looked around the table slowly and said, "Uncle Albert's planning another trip to California." She smiled, but it was kind of one of those smiles that she gives when she's going to give us extra work, or trouble. "And Aunt Beattie wants your sweater sizes again."

Chapter 28

The Student Council Meeting

I was the last one to arrive in the library for the student council meeting, but I had a good excuse. One of the first graders threw up during lunch, so I had take all of the other kids at his table outside while Joe cleaned the mess. And then it smelled so bad that we just sent all of the kids out to play early and opened all the doors and windows to air out the multipurpose room. So I had to watch them while I waited for the yard duty to come out. Who knew that the principal had to do all of this stuff? I sure didn't before I got the job. I told Paul later, and he said, "Yeah. Be a principal. Get food thrown at you and clean up vomit. Glad you got the job instead of me."

A lot of help he was. Anyway, I was about five minutes late to the meeting, and Gabe Sanchez, our vice president, had already started. Since he didn't have the agenda, they were just working on taking roll and checking out the posters for pajama day on Friday. We were planning to hang them up after lunch.

"Hi, sorry I'm late," I said.

"Oh, good. You're here," Gabe said, and then sat down.

"I hear Chrissy Miller threw up," Maddy said.

I just nodded and handed her the agendas. It was her job to hand them out. "Hi, Mrs. Kinney," I said, and gave her a copy.

She took the paper and started to read down it. Usually, it was about spirit days, like pajama day, or deciding who would do which job at the monthly awards assembly, or something like that. This one was different though, so she scowled at me.

"Billy, I thought this meeting was supposed to be about organizing the basketball club." That had been one of Gabe's ideas. Lots of kids liked to play basketball at lunch, and we were trying to get some kind of league formed, where kids would set up teams, and keep track of who won, and then have a tournament.

"Uh, let's wait until next meeting for that. I thought these things were more important."

She wasn't convinced. "These things are not really the job of the student council."

I just smiled. "When Principal Johnson's here, I agree, but since I'm principal, I decided that the student council should kind of change its role, at least for this week."

"Did you discuss this with Mr. Johnson?"

I flashed on my principal, dancing and doing back flips in his office while he sang the Oscar Meyer Wiener song. Did

I really think he was going to care if the student council worked on some of the school problems? I mean, it would just make less work for him when he got back, wouldn't it?

She folded her copy of the agenda and said, "Maybe we should end this meeting and wait for Mr. Johnson to come back."

All of the kids were looking at her now, and then they looked at me. "Well, since he made me principal, I think we'll still have the meeting, but if it will make you feel any better, I'll ask Mrs. Madigan to email him later."

She wasn't happy, but what could she say. After all, I was the principal, and if she didn't like it, she should go and eat lunch with the rest of the teachers while we had our meeting. She stood and said, "This is not the purpose of student council, and as the teacher representative to the student council, I'm afraid I'll have to end this meeting. You may go and hang your posters."

The kids looked at me. What was I going to do? I mean, I knew that some of the teachers were bothered that I was the principal, but nobody had really come right out and said we couldn't do what I wanted to do. On the other hand, I hadn't done anything different. Yet. Part of me thought I should just go along with what she wanted and let well enough alone, but part of me figured that if I was going to get blamed for all the problems and have to do all the principal work, I should get to do some good things too. So I just looked at her and said, "Well, Mrs. Kinney, if you don't want to be part of this meeting, you can go and have lunch, and we'll just have our meeting without you."

Remember when Mrs. Allistair slammed the door? Mrs. Kinney didn't do that, but I could tell that she sure wanted to. She stormed out of the library but just before she left, she pointed her finger at me. "Mr. Johnson will certainly hear about this!" she shouted. And then she stomped down the hall to the teacher's lunchroom.

Oh well. I'd known her since I had her for second grade and didn't really like her then either. She was mean, and full of herself, and really didn't teach us much. I turned back to the other kids. Maddy was the first to speak. "Should we just go out and hang the posters?"

"We have an agenda," I said.

Then one of the other kids said, "But I don't want to get in trouble."

Several others seemed to agree, and a couple even stood and reached for their posters.

"Wait just a minute here. We're the student council, the leaders of the school. Nothing in this agenda goes against any of that. Mrs. Kinney's just mad that we're not following her agenda." They hesitated, so I said, "Sit down. Let's look at it. Then if you don't think we should talk about those things, we'll go hang posters."

That seemed to work. Even the kids who were most worried about getting in trouble had to agree that just looking at the agenda wouldn't be a bad thing.

I stayed at the front. I was thinking. How could I do this? After about half a minute, I had an idea and called Maddy and Gabe and Muriel up front. They were the other officers, and I figured that we all had to stand together, even if they weren't sure yet. "Student Council Agenda, October 28th," I read. "Item one. Approval of minutes."

I looked over at Maddy. I knew the answer, but had to ask. "Maddy, did everybody get the minutes from the last meeting?" She nodded, so I looked out at the kids. They were starting to settle. "Any questions or changes?" When nobody spoke, I said, "In that case, all in favor of approving the minutes from the last meeting, raise your hand."

This was what we did at every meeting, and it seemed to help to get everybody back into the meeting mode. Every hand went up, and I said, "Motion passes. Maddy, you want to read the next item of business today?"

She looked at me, uncertain, and I nodded at her, so she cleared her throat and said, "Item Two. Student fights. No wonder Mrs. Kinney didn't like this."

"That's right," I said softly. "Student fights. Mr. Johnson and Mrs. Kinney and all the other adults complain that kids get in fights, but whatever they're doing about it, isn't working." I looked over at one of the fifth grade boys. "Alex, what happened when you got in a fight last week?"

He was startled, and a little embarrassed. "Uh, I didn't start it."

"I know you didn't, and it's over now. What happened?"

"Uh, I got sent to the office and they called my mom and told me to stay away from Jimmy Wallace."

"And what happened to Jimmy?"

"Same thing."

"He has to stay away from Jimmy Wallace?" I asked. "Sounds a little hard."

Everybody laughed and Alex said, "No. Me."

"So, you still mad at each other? You know why you started fighting?"

He shrugged his shoulders. "Sorta," he said.

"Sorta mad or sorta know why you were fighting?"

"Sorta both, I guess."

"So when you got sent to the office, and told not to see each other and your moms got called, did that solve the problem?"

He looked down at the floor now. "Not really. We kind of got in a shoving match on the way home from school yesterday."

"That's what I thought. Sorry to pick on you, Alex, but you were a perfect example." I scanned the room, making eye contact with every kid there. "This is what they've been doing for as long as I can remember, but all it does is stop the fight right now. It doesn't prevent the next fight." Some heads were nodding. Heck, we'd all been in fights, and I could tell that they were with me now, so I said, "My dad talks about how his company works on being proactive." They looked confused, so I wrote the word on the board. "It kind of means taking charge and acting before something happens."

"But how?" one of the kids asked.

I just grinned. "My sister's middle school had this system where if two kids got in a fight, other kids would run over to help."

"You mean they fight too?" one of the kids asked. He didn't really believe that was what I was thinking, but I guessed he might be confused.

"No. Help them calm down. Claire got in a fight with one of the other girls in her class, and they did that. Two other kids came over and asked if they needed help. They wear vests, kind of like the safety patrol, so everybody knows they're part of the Dispute Deputies. Claire and the other girl each got to tell their side of why they were fighting and the other had to listen. In the end, it was just a big misunderstanding and they both decided that fighting was kind of stupid."

"And that was the end of the fight," Muriel said softly. "I like that."

I'd come in with some other papers, and now I asked Maddy to hand them out. "When she was in eighth grade, my sister worked as one of the Dispute Deputies at her school. They lead the talking, and she's got a whole binder full of ideas. She even said that if I can get them out of school, she can probably get the Dispute Deputy kids to come in and help teach us what they do. Of course, that's if the student council wants me to ask her." Then I held up the page Maddy'd just handed out. "This is a short explanation. Take a look."

They read for the next minute or so. It was really just a series of cartoons of kids fighting, and then Dispute Deputies coming, and then talking and then shaking hands. When I could see that everyone was finished, I said, "Do you want me to ask her?"

Muriel leaned toward me and whispered, "You need a motion." She was our treasurer and parliamentarian, and it was her job to make sure that we did everything right.

I nodded. "Do I have a motion to invite my sister to our meeting?"

One of the fourth grade girls said, "I make a motion," and the girl next to her said, "I second the motion."

I grinned. "All in favor, raise your hands." Alex's hand shot into the air, and the others followed. "Good. I'll ask her tonight." Then I looked at Gabe. "You want to read item three?"

Gabe looked at the paper, and nodded. "Item Three. Homework Helpers."

"That's just what it says," I said, and then I told them of all of the parents I'd met with who were convinced that it was the teacher's fault, or the principal's fault that their kids were getting bad grades in school. I could see their disbelief. "It's true. I guess your parents are like mine. One bad call from the teacher, and I'm toast." Several of the kids nodded, and I said, "I talked with a couple of parents yesterday who told me that they can't help their kids with their homework because they don't get home from work until almost bedtime. So maybe it's time for kids to start helping kids." I wrote on the board, "Homework Helpers."

Then I read "Item Three. Wild Card." The others made sense, but this one was confusing, so I said, "You must have some other things you'd like to do to make the school better. Let's find one and get to work on that too." I looked at the clock. We only had about five minutes left, and I knew that we needed more time than that. I asked Gabe to run to the upper grade classrooms and tell the teachers that we were running late. As soon as he left, I said, "Here's what we're going to do..."

The student council actually had quite a few good wild card ideas, but then Maddy said, "I don't think we can do all of this by ourselves. We need to get more kids involved, so if nobody minds, let's change wild card to 'Assembly.' Maybe we can add some skits to Friday's awards assembly." Skits are fun, and everybody liked that, so we split into two groups, one for Dispute Deputies and the other for homework. We were pretty late by then, so we decided to meet the next day at lunch so that everyone could practice their skits.

You ever read about somebody having a spring in his step? My mom says sometimes when I'm really happy that I have a spring in my step. Well, I definitely bounced all the way back to Mr. Johnson's office.

Chapter 29

The Kindergarten Play

If I didn't think it could get any better after the student council meeting, I was wrong. Mrs. Gonzales, one of the kindergarten teachers, told me that they wanted to meet with me after school. What she really meant was that she wanted to meet with me after kindergarten, because the kindergarteners got out an hour before everyone else. I'm not sure why. I guess the teachers think the kids need to go home and take a nap, but I don't remember ever taking a nap in kindergarten. Hey, I know. Maybe the teachers need to go home and take a nap after spending all morning with a bunch of little kids. Now that makes a lot more sense.

She asked me to come half an hour early, so I went there right after I dropped the student council stuff off in my office. Oops, sorry. I meant Mr. Johnson's office. I must be spending too much time there. So I was running just to get from one place to the other, and on my way over there, I decided it was a good thing that I ate lunch with the little kids. I wonder how Mr. Johnson got so fat. It sure wasn't because it was easy to find time to eat. Maybe it was too many Oscar Meyer Wieners.

The kindergarten room is about half as big as the multipurpose room. It's huge. We have three kindergarten classes and they all fit inside, and that's a lot of little kids. And it isn't like the regular classrooms. There are no walls inside, just a big triangular building with a class in each corner, and teacher desks in the middle, and lots of room to play. I guess they built it that way so that the kids could get to know everybody else.

So I went in and the first thing I saw was that they'd taken one corner and set it up as a theater with a big curtain on a wooden stand for a stage and all of the kindergarten chairs set up facing the front. A lot of parents were there, and they were all trying to get comfortable in the little tiny kindergarten chairs, and I felt kind of sorry for them, because even my butt's too big for those things and I figured that some of the parents really needed two chairs. Then I hoped they wouldn't break any of them, because I was afraid that if they were too heavy and the chairs broke, that it would somehow end up being my fault since I was the principal.

Right after I got there, they dimmed the lights. Two of the parents had big flashlights, and they focused them on the curtain. While I watched, a couple of kids reached their hands out of the center and pulled the curtain open.

There were a bunch of other kids behind the curtain, all dressed up as animals with floppy ears and whiskers. They were really cute and I realized that I must have looked like that when I was in the kindergarten play. I couldn't remember the title, but it was something like the forest dance. And then they started to sing all about sunny days and butterflies and daisies, but it was kind of hard to see because of all the parents standing up and taking pictures. When they were done, one of the boys came running across the stage and stopped right in the middle in front of the singers and called, "Help! Sally Raccoon's fallen in the creek!" So the kids all got in a line and ran around in a circle, kind of like they were following a forest path. Then they went to the sides of the stage, and you could see that there was a big blue paper creek behind where the singers were and one of the girls, dressed like a raccoon, was laying right in the middle of it, waving her arms and legs back and forth and yelling, "Help!"

They all split up into small groups and tried to figure out how to get her out and every once in a while, somebody would yell out, "Throw her a branch," or "Try to get a rope to her," or something else, and you could tell that there were other kids at the sides, because when they threw the branch, it got pulled away along the blue paper. While that was happening, Sally Raccoon kept yelling, "Help!" and waving her arms. Finally, several of the kids held hands and formed a human chain and pulled her out. Once she was safely out of the blue paper, they all sang another song, and then I guess they were so happy that they all started dancing and some of the kids came out into the audience and grabbed their parents and danced with them. Two of the kids even came over to me and I had to dance too. The whole show only lasted about fifteen minutes, but it was lots of fun, and it made me remember that sometimes I really miss kindergarten.

After the play was over, the bell rang and the parents took their kids home. Then the teachers waved me over to one of the little tables and had me sit in a kindergarten chair. Since they were all sitting in little tiny chairs too, I couldn't complain much.

Mrs. Gonzales started. "So how do you like being the principal, Billy?"

She was my old kindergarten teacher, and one of my mom's friends, and we still waved when we saw each other. "It has its ups and downs," I said. When I saw them frown I said, "But I definitely liked watching the kids in the play."

They all liked that, and talked about how good Sally Raccoon was, and how much work it had been to teach them the songs, and did I enjoy dancing? Evidently that had been Mrs. Gonzales' idea.

Then she said, "We're going to need more fabric for the costumes for the next play."

Uh huh, I nodded. So what did that have to do with me?

Then one of the teachers opened up some kind of magazine. "I found just the patterns we need in this catalog. She showed it to me. It looked like lots of pictures of cloth with designs that looked like zebras and leopards and giraffes. Then they all looked at me like I needed to do something.

"Uh, those look good."

"It'll be an African theme," Mrs. Gonzales said. "We have a team of parents all lined up to sew the costumes."

I still wasn't sure what they wanted, and then I got it. They wanted the school to pay for the fabric. Could we do that? Then I thought about Mr. Johnson's signature stamp. I could buy just about anything with that, which got me thinking that a new iPad might be a nice reward for being principal, but I was getting distracted so I just said, "You want the school to buy it, right?"

"And buttons and zippers and ribbon and velcro," one of them said.

"Well, I don't know much about ordering stuff, but Mrs. Madigan should be able to take care of it for you."

"So we have your approval?" Mrs. Gonzales asked.

I just shrugged my shoulders. "Sure."

Chapter 30

Revolting Teachers

Actually, Mr. Ward says that's not a very good name for this chapter. I had him read it and he said that revolting really has two meanings. Did I tell you that Mr. Ward was helping with my book? I'll bet I forgot that. It was his idea. He told me when I first got assigned to be principal that I had to keep a journal about my experience. It was part of my homework, and it wasn't much fun at the time with everything else I had to do, but now I can look back at all of the weird things that happened.

Anyway, he said that revolting could mean that the teachers were fighting against something I wanted to do, and after talking to Mrs. Kinney, I guess that some of them were pretty angry about my student council agenda. They seem to think that only teachers can have good ideas about stopping fights and helping kids with homework. So they were revolting and telling me that I couldn't do that because I'm just a kid.

According to Mr. Ward though, revolting has another

meaning, and he's afraid some people might get upset when they read my chapter title, because they might think I mean the teachers are revolting, meaning really disgusting. So I talked to him about it, and then decided to keep the title the way it is. After all, it is my book, so I get to do those things. Then I decided that maybe I should add this explanation, just in case you might be confused. Of course, part of me thinks that their revolt was a little revolting, if you get that.

Anyway, after I met with the kindergarten teachers, I told Mrs. Madigan that they wanted to order fabric for costumes and that they'd see her about it and that as soon as the order was ready, I'd stamp it with Mr. Johnson's stamp. She kind of frowned, but I guess that she figured it was okay since I was the principal.

I went back to Mr. Johnson's office, and there was nobody there, so I got busy on my homework. I was working on dividing some mixed numbers when I heard a knock on the door. I turned around, and Mrs. Kinney was standing there. Her arms were crossed and she was thumping her foot on the floor and my first thought was, "Uh oh. I'm in big trouble now." Then I thought, for what? For being the student council president and writing the agenda? That was my job.

"Can we come in?" she said, but even before she finished, she was standing in the middle of the room and Mr. Ward and Mrs. Lowenhurst, a fourth grade teacher, were standing right behind her.

"Uh, sure," I said. I put my paper and pencil on my math book, and then I turned my chair back to them. I could see Mr. Ward had a little bit of a smile on his face and I figured it had to be because I was doing my homework.

"We want to talk about your agenda at the student council meeting today," Mrs. Kinney said.

"Yes," Mrs. Lowenhurst said. "Doris, I mean Mrs. Kinney, showed it to the teachers in the staff room and we're not sure it's appropriate for student council."

Uh oh. I tried to think of what my parents would do if they had three angry teachers trying to talk to them. Dad always said that the best thing to do was to listen, partly to hear what the people had to say, and partly just to give yourself time to figure out what you need to do. I'd used that strategy once when a group of middle school boys tried to take away our basketball court at the park and it seemed to work pretty well then, so I decided that I'd just stay silent.

And the silence stretched. And stretched. Finally, Mrs. Kinney said, "Well?"

I looked at her. "Well, what?"

Now she was rattled. "Well, do you think it was appropriate for the student council?"

"Yes. If I hadn't thought it was appropriate, I wouldn't have written it." Then I went silent again. They were going to have to tell me why having kids helping other kids with homework or trying to prevent fights was a bad idea.

"It is not what the student council does," Mrs. Kinney said, and the other two nodded.

I thought for a moment. "I agree that it's not what the student council usually does, but then so far as I know, the student council president was never the principal before either."

"What's that got to do with anything?" Mrs. Kinney asked. "Are you trying to say that just because Mr. Johnson did something stupid, you get to change the way this school is run?"

Ah, so they were mad because Mr. Johnson made me the principal. I still thought it was a good idea to stay pretty quiet, so I just looked at them. I really didn't think that Mrs. Kinney expected an answer to her question anyway. She was still thumping her foot, but Mr. Ward was trying to look over my shoulder, probably to see what problem I was on, and I figured he'd just come along to support the others, but my agenda didn't really bother him. After all, he was the one who knew me best and the only one who could really give me detention. And then I heard it. Mrs. Lowenhurst was growling. When I was in fourth grade, and she taught fifth, Max told me that her nickname was "Growler," because when she was mad at the class she kind of growled. I started to grin, but then decided that would be a bad idea and I actually bit my tongue so hard to keep from laughing that it really hurt.

And for some reason that made me think about what my sister said about people constantly trying to give you their monkeys, and when I looked at the teachers in front of me, I could tell that was exactly what they were trying to do, only they didn't really want to. Here I was, the Student Council President, offering to try to take the homework monkey and the fighting monkey away from them, but they didn't want to give them up, maybe because they were afraid kids might have some good ideas, but maybe just because they liked their monkeys. Wow! This was so confusing and weird that my head was starting to hurt. Then I realized that I was still biting my tongue, so I relaxed a bit. I looked back at them.

Mrs. Kinney was trying to stare right through me. She said, "Maybe you forgot that I'm the Student Council Advisor and everything you do has to be approved by me."

"No," I said, "I haven't forgotten." But by now I was getting kind of mad. We had talked about helping kids not to fight and to do their homework. What could be better than that? So I was feeling pretty good about what student council was doing and that was when I made my mistake. I reminded her that I was the principal, and while the Student Council Advisor got to approve what happened at student council, the principal got to approve what the student council advisor did.

Uh oh. I knew as soon as I said it that she wouldn't like that, and boy was I right. She didn't like that at all. In fact, she started thumping her foot so hard that Mrs. Madigan came in to see if we were having an earthquake. Or maybe she came in to see who'd let in a wild bear, because Mrs. Lowenhurst was really growling loudly now. Mrs. Kinney crumpled up the paper she was holding and said, "Well, this is what I think of your agenda!" And then she threw it at me. Can you imagine what would have happened if one of her kids had done that with their homework in her class? Yeah. Not a pretty picture. Detention until they had grey hair.

But it really didn't bother me that much, because that paper was the agenda for the last meeting, the one that was already over, not the next one that we were having at lunch tomorrow. Still, I figured I'd kind of said the wrong thing, so I took a deep breath and reached down to pick up the paper, and then put it on my desk and smoothed it out. That's when I saw that she'd used a yellow highlighter to underline fight and homework. Interesting. I guess that was so that the other teachers would see just how wrong I'd been without having to read the whole thing.

Then I thought of another trick my parents had taught me. When everybody is mad at you, be humble. So I just shrugged my shoulders and smiled. "Actually, we were planning to take a part of Friday's assembly to talk with the kids about Dispute Deputies and Homework Club." I didn't tell her that was Maddy's idea, because Maddy was in her class, and I figured she'd be guaranteed to get in trouble if Mrs. Kinney knew she was one of my co-conspirators.

They all stared at me and Mrs. Lowenhurst growled, and said, "That's an awards assembly."

"I know, but Mr. Johnson always has other stuff going on during the awards assemblies."

She just said, "Harrumph!" but she couldn't say much more than that because it was true. Mr. Johnson talked about fundraisers and had a whole program where kids used skits to teach about manners in class and the lunchroom, and other stuff like that. This was pretty much the same.

"So I'll just be following his example," I said. Then I acted like I'd just had a really good idea. "Say, we were talking about organizing our assembly skits tomorrow at lunch time. Maybe you'd like to come and help." Really, I didn't want their help, but I figured that if I offered and they said no, then they couldn't complain as much about me taking over and doing stuff only teachers were allowed to do, like helping kids with homework.

Mrs. Kinney snarled at me. "I don't have time to have lunch with a bunch of kids two days this week. I have work to do."

Mrs. Lowenhurst just growled for a while. Finally, she said, "Student council is not my responsibility."

Hmm. The ones who were complaining the most were the ones who were just too busy to help out. I felt like I was back in kindergarten where everybody wanted to play but some kids didn't want to help when it was time to clean up. Then Mr. Ward said, "Billy, that sounds like a good compromise. Where will you be meeting?"

The other two teachers shot their heads around and stared at him like he was some kind of teacher traitor, but I didn't want them to have a chance to say anything, so I said, "In the library. Thanks for offering to help."

"Good," he said. "I'm looking forward to it." He smiled and added, "Now I'd better run. I have to get ready for tomorrow." And before anybody could say anything else, he turned around and headed out of the office.

I heard him say hello to Mrs. Madigan just before Mrs. Kinney turned to Mrs. Lowenhurst and said, "Well, he never was much of a team player." And without even saying goodbye, or hope you don't have to stay up too late with your math homework, or how's your mom, or anything else, they stomped right out of the office. Yep. Just like kindergarteners. And then I started to laugh. Finally. I'd been holding it in for way too long. I laughed at the growling and thumping feet, and the monkeys, and even Mrs. Kinney throwing my agenda paper at me, but mostly because they didn't think Mr. Ward was much of a team player. I don't think they even understood that he'd just decided to join my team!

Chapter 31

Walking Home

I stayed and worked on my homework for a while after that even though school was out. I figured I had time, because Wednesday was Danny's Art Club day. That was where a group of third grade parents run an art club and the kids get to stay after school and make things like ceramic animals and other stuff. It usually lasts for an hour, which was enough time for me to stay and get most of my homework done. In the past, I just stayed at my desk in Mr. Ward's classroom, but since I had an office now, I stayed there.

At 4:00, he showed up at the door. "Hi," he said, and looked around. I'd been principal for a week by now, but he hadn't had a chance to poke around in the principal's office much yet. He looked over at two chairs against the wall. They were smaller than Mr. Johnson's chair, so he asked, "Is that where Mr. Johnson makes the bad kids sit?" I nodded and he looked at me. "Do the kids get sent to you too?"

"I guess," I said. "I've had a couple each day. Usually we just talk a little bit about what they're supposed to be doing in class, and I send them back, and remind them that since they got in trouble in class, they have to sit at table eight, or pick up garbage at lunch time. A couple were really mad, so I made them just stay there for a while until they cooled down."

Danny sat now, trying out one of the chairs. "What were they mad about?"

I shrugged my shoulders, as if to say, 'What are kids usually mad about, their teachers.' Then I said it.

He surprised me by nodding in agreement and adding, "Yeah. That's what I'd guess. That and arguments with other kids, but mostly being mad at the teachers."

"So how would you know all that," I asked, "You never get in trouble."

"Doesn't mean I don't watch. It seems like usually the kids who get sent to the office just can't sit still, or get bored and start talking to somebody else, or something like that. And sometimes they get sent for doing something that we didn't even know was against the rules."

Huh. I was starting to figure that out from talking to kids who got sent in to see me. How'd Danny get so smart? Then I thought about Mr. Ward, and Mrs. Anderson, the teacher I had in fifth grade. They hardly ever sent anyone to the office, and that was usually for a fight on the playground. I wondered why, and then I got it. Even when we were working on grammar, or memorizing multiplication facts, or something boring like that, their classes were fun, and we all knew the rules. Then I remembered that Mrs. Mckenzie almost never sent anyone to the office either, and her class could be deadly boring sometimes, but everybody was careful with her because her rules were so strict. Huh. I looked at Danny. Two of the kids in his class had been sent to the office for goofing off in class today, and a couple of different ones on Monday. And his teacher was Mrs. Lowenhurst, the growler.

"So how was Mrs. Lowenhurst today?"

He gave me a big theatrical yawn and said, "How is Mrs. Lowenhurst every day?" Then he laughed. "Boy is she mad at you! I was afraid for a while that she'd give me extra homework, or maybe a detention, but she didn't."

I asked quietly, "Why's she mad at me?"

"I guess Mrs. Kinney's one of her friends, and she talked to her about student council. All the kids are talking about how you smacked her down."

"Mrs. Kinney? I didn't..." And then I thought. Did Mrs. Kinney think I'd smacked her down? I looked at Danny. "Kids are talking about that?"

"Oh yeah. Some of the kids, anyway. I'm kind of a celebrity just because you're my brother."

"I didn't really smack her down," I said carefully.

"I know. Maddy told me what happened, but as far as Mrs. Kinney is concerned, you did."

I didn't say anything while I packed my books and papers into my backpack. I just had a different agenda than what she was used to, that's all, and when she told me she didn't like it, I didn't back down. But hey, what's wrong with trying to help kids with homework, or stopping fights? We wouldn't need a different plan if her system worked.

Then I started to grin. "She really thinks I smacked her down?"

"Yep."

I stood up. "Ready to walk home?"

While we walked home, Danny and I talked about what had happened both in the library and later in the office with the Thumper and the Growler. Danny laughed at the nicknames, because his fourth grade friends told him that Mrs. Kinney thumped her foot when she was upset in class too. Then he asked a couple of questions that really got me thinking about the meeting tomorrow at lunch time, and how I might use that to pull the kids together and get the teachers' approval at the same time. Did I mention that my brother's a pretty smart guy?

Chapter 32

The Assembly

By eleven o'clock on Friday morning, we had finished the primary grade assembly. I had fun standing up front with the class teachers and helping to give out awards. I had even more fun when I got to give out the bumper stickers for "Citizen of the Month." The kids were really jazzed, and most of their parents were there, hiding behind the door into the kitchen so that they could come running out when the kid got up to the stage. A lot of them thanked me, like I had something to do with their kid being a good citizen, and a few of them even told me that they were really glad that I was doing such a good job as the student principal. That felt really good. I certainly wasn't hearing that from Mrs. Kinney or the parents of the kids who got into trouble. And that got me thinking that maybe the way to get the teachers on my side was to give them awards, or even better, to give them awards and hide their moms and dads in the kitchen so that they could come running out and give them a big hug. After all, I could tell that Mom still liked it when Grandma gave her a big hug and told her she was proud of her and you would think that Mom's pretty old for that kind of stuff.

The most fun was giving out the permission slips for the pizza party. Mr. Johnson had this system where each teacher got to nominate two kids who had worked really hard in class for the past month, and those kids got to eat lunch with the principal. I'd gotten that a few times, and it was fun, and I guess maybe I'd learned a lot about being a principal there. The first graders all figured they'd be eating lunch with me, and I couldn't convince them that Mr. Johnson would be back by next Friday. By third grade though, they knew I was just a temporary fill in, so they said thanks, and a couple asked if they'd be eating with the real principal.

Michael, remember Michael, the kid who got in a fight my first day as principal? Well, he got an award for being most improved over the past week. Interesting. And when I gave him the award, he whispered to me that he was one of the kids who helped Max with the clean up after the food fight. Who'd have guessed that?

Well, the little kids left and I took a minute to get a drink of water, and then the older kids came in. They all got settled, and I watched the sixth graders sit along the wall on the benches. Then Mrs. Kinney came up front and handed me her awards, since fourth graders got their awards first. That's when I said, "We're going to start with the student council program."

That really wasn't much of a change, since Mr. Johnson usually did his stuff first, before awards, but she looked at me like I was being really disrespectful. "We have lots of awards to give out."

"We have time," I said. "The primary kids are going to

have a picnic on the field today, so if we run late, they'll be outside anyway." Then I smiled. And she smiled, but her smile was kind of a sick thing that said she'd really prefer to slap me with her awards folder.

The picnic on the lawn was one of Mr. Ward's ideas. He told us that he heard that Mrs. Kinney and a couple of the other teachers were planning to take so long with their awards that we wouldn't have time for the student council skits before the primary lunch started, so I should make sure that the skits went first.

So Mrs. Kinney went back to her class. When she got there, she sat next to Mrs. Mckenzie and whispered something over to her, but I didn't really pay much attention, because it was my time to speak.

"Welcome to the October Awards Ceremony everyone. It's nice to see so many people wearing their pajamas." I nodded toward a couple of teachers who were sitting in their bathrobes. "Teachers too!" I hadn't been sure if I should wear pajamas to school, since I was the principal, but Mom had convinced me that I was a sixth grader first, and needed to show my school spirit, so I had. There were lots of laughs and cheers. When it got quiet, I continued. "First, I want to thank everybody here for their hard work all month." It was the same thing Mr. Johnson always started with. "I have a couple of announcements that Mrs. Madigan asked me to share with you." I referred to my notes. "Parent conferences are coming up in November and she wants to be sure that you take home the sign-up forms today. Also, since it's such a warm sunny day, we'll be eating lunch outside on the lawn. And finally, your fund raiser packages are due back to your teachers by the end of next week." I stepped away from the microphone and waved to Maddy. "Your Student Council Vice President will take over from here. We have a couple of skits for you today."

There was a round of cheers, but I knew they weren't for me. Skits were always popular.

Maddy walked over to the front. She was a little nervous, because she'd only been vice president for a couple of months and was only a fourth grader, and didn't do much speaking, but we'd been practicing, so she was ready. Then she started to speak, but nothing came out. I was on the side, and I could see her lips moving and all, but there was no sound. She tried again, but I still couldn't hear anything, so I ran up to her. "You okay?"

"I don't think this works," she said, and held out the microphone to me. Meantime, the kids were starting to talk, and a few were laughing.

"Sorry. I must have turned it off." I turned it back on again and tapped the top and it made a loud popping sound. Then I turned it off again and whispered to her, "I still couldn't hear you from the side. Talk loudly and hold it up to your lips." I turned the microphone back on, tapped it again to make sure it was working, and then raised my hand in the silent attention signal. Maddy's and most of the kids' went up as well, and within just a few seconds, it was quiet.

"Sorry," she said. Then she looked down. Other student council kids were standing below the front of the stage, holding signs.

 Seeing all of us supporting her seemed to give her courage, and she said in a loud, clear voice, "We have four sets of skits for you today, and then we'll be asking for your help to set up a couple of new programs here at W. H. Carpenter School. Your student council has been working on these, and we think they'll be great for kids and good for teachers too." That was one of the things Mr. Ward suggested as a concession to teachers to get them behind the new ideas, and make them see that it would help them too, even though the ideas came from kids.

"First, we want to talk about homework." There were some boos, most of them coming from the sixth graders. Mrs. Wilson and Mr. Ward gave their classes their meanest teacher looks, and they quieted down. "So," she went on, "the way homework works now." She waved her hand and a bunch of kids ran out onto the stage. "After each little mini skit, my lovely assistants will hold up their signs. If you think this is a good situation, clap for the happy face." One of the girls held up a sign with a large round happy face on it. "If you think it's a bad situation, clap for the sad face." A boy held up a large round sign with a sad face on it.

Then Maddy said, "Now on with the show." She stepped to the side and the kids could see one girl was sitting at a desk, writing on a piece of paper. "Oh, no," she said loudly enough for everyone in the room to hear, "I just don't understand how to do my homework." She looked at the clock on the wall and then shook her head sadly, "and my mom doesn't get home from work until nine o'clock. By then it'll be too late." She sighed loudly. "I'm going to get detention for sure."

Maddy stepped forward and said into the mike, "Happy?" The kid with the happy face held it up high. Most kids were quiet, but a few that my parents would have called smart alecks started to clap wildly, at least until their teachers saw them. "Or sad." Quite a few kids clapped this time. Good, they were starting to get it.

Then the kids with the signs crouched down and another kid on the stage was talking with a kid who was dressed up as the dorkiest looking teacher I'd ever seen. She had this dull plaid dress and a long grey wig with a bow in it, and old fashioned glasses that hung on a chain around her neck. "I'm sorry I didn't get my homework done. My little brother is really wild when I get home and it's too noisy to be able to concentrate."

The kid who was dressed as a teacher said in a nasty voice, "No excuses. You get detention, detention, detention!" Then she jumped up and down, cackling like an evil witch while she wagged her finger at him. The kids all laughed, but when the signs went up, the cheers went for the sad face.

The last skit was a boy who was standing in front of a girl who was dressed as a teacher with big round glasses, and standing on a chair so that the boy had to look way up to her. "I don't have my homework," he said, and hung his head, "my dog ate it." The kids laughed again, and the girl in the chair waited until they stopped and said, "Well, I guess you'll have to do it over again during detention. Maybe you can get your dog to help." He sighed and walked sadly off the stage.

That one with the dog was my idea. It wasn't really the kind of thing that we could solve with a homework club, but one of my friends really did have his dog eat his homework one time. Really. No, really. If you'd ever met his dog, you'd understand. I think he was eating his snack after school and he got some peanut butter on his math paper and his dog just gobbled it up. So there went half an hour of homework down the drain, or down the dog, I guess. And he still got detention even though his mom wrote a note saying the dog ate his homework. I guess if we had a homework club, at least he'd have a place to do it over.

Then another boy stood up. He was rubbing his chin, like he was really confused, or something, and said, "Gee, I really don't understand my math homework, and there won't be anybody at home to help me. I guess maybe I'll go to homework club after school." Then he smiled and walked off the stage. I could tell the kids in the audience were a little confused, because they really didn't say anything, but there was a little applause for the happy face.

And then another couple of kids stood up and one said to the other, "Are you going to homework club after school?"

The other one said, "I sure am. I like getting my homework done before I go home." Some more kids clapped for the happy face.

Two more kids stood up. One said, "What are you doing after school today?"

The other one answered her, "I'm going to homework club. I really like helping the little kids with their homework."

The first one said, "Me too!" Then they started to walk off the stage, talking about homework club. The kids watching the skit were starting to get it now, so there was more clapping for the happy face.

Maddy came back out onto the stage. "So that's our first new student council idea. We want to start an after school homework club where kids help kids to get their homework done. Your student council representatives will tell you more about this when they make their reports in the classroom. We'll be looking for some people to volunteer to help the little kids, or even sixth graders to help fifth graders or other sixth graders." She looked over at me and I walked to the center of the stage.

I took the microphone. "Thanks, Maddy. That was great." Then I asked for a big round of applause for all of our actors. When it quieted down, I said, "We talked about another idea in student council too, kids fighting." I looked down. Everybody was listening except for a few of the same kids who were cheering at the wrong time before. Mrs. Kinney just gave me a nasty look, but most of the teachers looked interested. "My dad says that getting in fights is just part of being a kid, but solving problems shows you're growing up." Then I turned toward the stage and pointed.

Two boys came out from opposite sides. When they got close, one made a point of bumping the other with his shoulder. The boy who got bumped said, "Hey. Quit hitting me."

The second boy said, "I didn't hit you."

Then the first pushed the other boy and said. "You trying to start a fight?" And then they started pushing back and forth on the stage. A few of the kids in the audience started yelling, "Fight, fight!" until they looked at their teachers and got quiet.

Then another kid came running over. She was the same

one dressed as the really dorky teacher, and she said, "Hey, no fighting." The two boys backed away a little bit but gave each other angry looks as the teacher kid stood between them with her arms held wide to keep them from starting again. "I'm sending you both to the principal."

One of the kids said, "It was his fault," and the other said, "I didn't do anything." Then I walked out onto the stage. I was wearing one of my dad's neckties. Yeah, it looked really stupid over my pajamas, but Mom thought it'd be a good addition to the uniform. She even tied it and then loosened it up so that I could just slip it over my head. "Have you been fighting?" I yelled. Both boys hung their heads, acting really sorry. "Well, I guess you can both eat at table eight tomorrow and then pick up garbage all during lunch, but first I'm going to call your parents.

One boy said, "No. Not that. My dad's gonna whip me."

I gave him an evil look. "Good," I said.

The kids below jumped up with their signs. First, the sad face and lots of applause. Nobody clapped for the happy face.

As soon as the applause stopped, I looked out at the kids in the audience. "Or, we could do it this way."

The two boys took their places on the sides of the stage. They walked toward each other. They bumped, they complained, and they started pushing and shoving. Suddenly, two kids in orange safety patrol vests ran to the boys. One of them said, "Hey, no fighting." The boys looked at them and then pulled apart, just like before. Then one safety patrol kid said, "You want to talk about it or do you want us to call a teacher?"

The two fighters kind of glared at each other, and then snarled, "Talk."

The other safety patrol kid said, "Ok. Here are the rules. You take turns telling what happened, but no interrupting. You can't touch each other and you can't call names. Can you do that?"

One boy looked at the other and grumbled, "I don't want a teacher."

"Me neither," said the other.

Then the first safety patrol kid said, "Ok, you first. What happened?"

The boy said, "I was just walking along when he hit me."

The other kid's face lit up and he tried to interrupt but the safety patrol kid held up her hand and said, "You have to listen. You'll get your turn." So he looked at the other boy who just repeated what he'd already said. Finally, the girl said, "Ok. Are you done?" When he nodded, she turned to the other boy. "Now you tell me what happened."

He said, "Well he bumped into me first."

They talked for a minute or so, until one of the safety patrol kids said, "Do you think it could have been an accident?" Both boys nodded and she said, "So do you want to shake hands and be done with the fight or do you want me to call a teacher?"

"Be done," one said and the other nodded. So they shook hands and one of the boys who'd been fighting said, "Do you want to go play basketball?" Then they both ran off the stage. This time, when the happy face went up, there was a lot of applause.

I came back to the stage. I could see a lot of the kids were excited, but what really looked good to me was that most of the teachers were smiling and nodding too. Well, not Mrs. Kinney or Mrs. Mckenzie or Mrs Lowenhurst. They were scowling, but I think it was because they were worried that they wouldn't be able to give as many detentions if kids solved their own problems. I think maybe they kept score, like some kind of contest, and then the wining teacher got a prize at the end of the week.

I raised the microphone to my lips. "They used this in my sister's middle school. The kids in the vests get training and are called Dispute Deputies. From what she said, the kids really liked it, and it cut way down on fights." Then I scanned the teachers, "Oh, and the teachers like it too, because they only have to get involved in the big fights where the kids are too mad to listen, so it saves them a lot of time." That was my award for the teachers. I know they're pretty busy, so I figured they had to like anything that would save them work. Well, maybe not Mrs. Kinney or Mrs. Mckenzie or Mrs. Lowenhurst.

"So," I continued, "Student council will be looking for volunteers to help with this too. If you're interested, let your representative know. I'm going to try to get some of the middle school kids to come over here to help train us at this school. I guess visiting other schools is one of the things that they do." Then I called all of the student council actors up to the stage and everybody took a big bow. The audience cheered.

When we did awards, Mr. Ward gave me the Citizen of the Month award. I was really surprised, and really glad when my mom and dad came running out from the kitchen, because I could wipe some tears on my mom's blouse when they hugged me. Then I made a big deal out of handing the award to myself and thanking myself for doing such a good job. It was kind of hard to shake hands with myself while I was still holding the award, but I managed. Even Mrs. Kinney laughed at that.

Chapter 33

Retirement Again (I Hope!)

School got out at three o'clock, and by three-thirty, the busses were gone, and the kids were gone, and even most of the teachers were gone. Danny was playing basketball with a couple of friends when I walked out to the playground. "You ready to walk home?" I called.

He shot one more shot, and watched as it bounced off the rim. Then he came running over. His first words were, "I liked the skits. You really think you can do that stuff?"

I shrugged my shoulders. "I hope so. Even if I'm not principal next week, I'll still be Student Council President. I guess I'll have to talk it over with Mr. Johnson."

When we got home, Mom said, "Oh, good. I'm glad to see you boys. How was school?"

"Okay." I said. I really just wanted to get some juice and a snack, not talk about assemblies and stuff like that. Then I thought about the kindergarten skit. I hadn't mentioned it before. "The kindergarteners did a play yesterday and I got to go see it."

"Oh, that's nice," she said. "I always enjoyed watching you kids in the kindergarten plays." But she really wasn't paying too much attention, so I just opened the refrigerator and tried to take out a soda instead of juice, but she caught me and shook her head. I guess I wasn't the principal at home.

She said, "Danny, why don't you open the mail, and then I'd like you to write that letter to Aunt Beattie." He looked at me, and rolled his eyes. I was really glad that I didn't have the mailman job any more. And then I laughed. Not only did he have the mailman job, there weren't any younger kids to take over when he hit sixth grade. He was stuck forever.

I put the juice on the table for later, and took my backpack to my room. It felt really, really good to just be a kid again.

Chapter 34

Mr. Johnson Quits

On Monday morning, Mr. Ward had me take the roll sheet to the office again. I thought he should probably share the job with somebody else, but he seemed to think it was really funny to ask me if I knew my way to the office.

I guess he'd been planning this with the kids in the class, because one of them said, "And can you tell the lunch ladies that we need more taco sauce on the tacos?"

Another one said, "And my bus was late getting me home last week. Can you take care of that?"

One of the girls laughed and said, "One of the girls in the other sixth grade class was calling me names this weekend. Can you give her detention?"

I just gave them a sick smile and walked out the door. When I got to the office, Mrs. Madigan was waiting for me. I handed her the roll sheet and she handed me another email. I looked at the top of it and could see that it was from Elmer Johnson. Why would he be sending her an email? He should be in his office. I could feel a big weight settling into my stomach, like maybe I'd eaten too many donuts for breakfast. I looked at her and she nodded. Then I began to read.

Mrs. Madigan,

I have great news. The producer of America's Most Amazing Acts liked my personality so well that he's offered me a job as a full time judge on the show. I'm starting Monday! In fact, they're going to pay me about five times what I was making as a principal. I'll be moving to LA as soon as possible.

I talked to Superintendent Williams last night and she said that the school district would get right to work on hiring a new principal. For now, please thank Billy for doing such a good job as principal while I've been gone. I'm sure he will be happy to fill in until they find my replacement.

Elmer

I looked over at Mrs. Madigan. She was watching to see if I had any reaction. I think my only reaction was to look like I was going to throw up. Then she smiled. I couldn't believe it. Here I was, feeling like I was going to jail or something and she just smiled. "I'm happy to have you back, Billy, even if it's only for this morning."

"Yeah," I said. "I guess I'll go get my stuff." I felt like I just didn't have any energy at all. I mean, if I was going to be principal, we could start the homework club and Dispute Deputy programs, but I really missed being a sixth grader. I started to trudge toward my classroom. Then, just as I was going out the back door, I stopped. "Whoa! What do you mean, only for this morning?"

She giggled. I'd never heard Mrs. Madigan giggle before. It sounded like somebody had just told her the world's greatest joke. She said, "I wondered if you'd caught that. You get to go back to class after lunch. Mrs. Gonzalez will take over after that."

I was confused. "Mrs. Gonzales? The kindergarten teacher?"

"That's right," she said. "She used to be a principal in one of the other schools, so Mrs. Williams called her up last night and asked her to take over for the rest of the year. They couldn't get a substitute for her class today, so she'll take over after her kids go home."

"You mean, I get to go back to just being a sixth grader?"

She giggled again, and this time I could tell that she was just happy for me. "That's right."

"Whoohoo!" I yelled. I'm not sure my feet touched the ground all the way back to class.

When I got there, Mr. Ward said, "I put your homework assignments on your desk."

I just looked at him. He already knew. How'd that happen?

He came over and patted me on the back. "Mrs. Gonzales called me last night and asked for you for just one more day. See you this afternoon."

Chapter 35

Aftermath

OK. I'd better explain this title too. It kind of sounds like the chapter that starts after math is over and you go on to reading or science or something, but aftermath really means what happens after the other stuff. See how it's just one word, even if it sounds like two? English is kind of a crazy language that way. So, you got it? Not after math, but aftermath.

Anyway, Mrs. Gonzales kept me in the office for the rest of the day, and called me in several times over the next two weeks. I didn't mind though, since mostly she just wanted to know about some of the things I'd done.

I showed her the book orders for next year, and the fabric order for kindergarten, and a lot of other stuff, and then she told me that she'd heard about the homework club idea and the Dispute Deputies program and really liked both of them. So that was why we had so many meetings. We had a lot of work to do to get those going.

Mrs. Kinney resigned as the teacher in charge of Student

Council. She said that she just couldn't imagine working with rude students who didn't respect her opinions. That was just fine with me, because it was true. I really didn't respect her opinions at all.

The even better part though, was when Mr. Ward volunteered to take over from her. He said he'd been trying to get the Dispute Deputies program going for the past couple of years, but Mr. Johnson didn't want to take the time, so it didn't go anywhere. Now though, he figured that since the student council was all ready to do the work, and parents and even most of the teachers were excited about it, he'd like to help by setting up the trainings with the middle school kids. Did I tell you he taught my sister in seventh grade? Really. He was at the middle school, and was in charge of the Dispute Deputies program there too!

Mrs. Mckenzie volunteered to help with homework club. I know. I was amazed too. I mean Mrs. Mckenzie was the queen of homework detention. But it turned out that she thought that having kids help other kids to get their homework done was a really good idea. And she had some really good ideas of her own, like we could use the library where kids could get books if they had to, and she was going to ask parents to help supervise so that we could make sure kids were really doing homework instead of just playing around. Then she had another idea that I wasn't so sure about, but the teachers liked it, so it helped to get them excited about something that came from student council. The kids wanted to have a homework club where kids could kind of drop in and get help. Mrs. Mckenzie thought teachers should be able to assign kids to homework club too. I guess the more I thought about it, the more it made sense, but it sure meant that some of the kids might not want to be there.

So it was a pretty good couple of weeks, and we got lots of things done, but that wasn't the exciting part. No, that wasn't anywhere near the exciting part.

Mrs. Gonzales decided that having a drawing to get pizza for just a couple of kids who worked hard every month was leaving out a lot of other kids who worked just as hard, or sometimes even harder, so she decided that instead of pizza, she'd have a popsicle party after lunch one Friday each month. And she told the student council that we had to come to the popsicle party every time, so that we could work on getting kids really excited about student council for next year, which meant that student council kids got popsicles every month.

But even that wasn't the best part. She also wanted us there with the other kids at the popsicle parties because she said that kids were really smart, and they had lots of good ideas that could help the school, like Homework Club and Dispute Deputies, and she wanted us to see what other good ideas we might have.

But that wasn't the best part either, not even close. The best part, and you're really going to like this, because I really like it and I'm the one writing this story, so if you like the story, you have to agree with me. The best part was the popsicles. That's right, the popsicles. Mrs. Gonzales found a company that made popsicles that was called 'Billy's Popsicles,' and she called the popsicle party Billy's Popsicle Day. Now is that cool or what!

Chapter 36

Uncle Albert Returns

I was the first one to see Uncle Albert getting off of the train. He looked pretty much the same as he had before, the same green and yellow checked jacket, the same yellow tennis shoes, and even the same white shirt with the stain on the front. In fact, he even had the same paisley bow tie and the hat with the green feather in it.

We all walked up to him and I took his suitcase. Yep, the same one. I took a look at it, wondering if it was full of ugly green and yellow sweaters. I couldn't tell, but there couldn't be much more in there.

"So how was your trip, Uncle Albert?" Mom asked.

"Always lovely," he said. "Nothing like a good ride on the train."

"Why don't you fly?" I asked.

"What, and miss all of that beautiful scenery." He shook his head. "No, the train's the only way to travel."

I thought about his trip across Nevada. What beautiful

scenery? Have you ever driven across Nevada? It's just brownish grey hills as far as you can see for hour after hour after hour. Maybe he takes a different route, but I doubt it. Maybe it looks different through train windows.

We were walking out to the car now, and he asked, "Where's Claire?"

"She's skating with her friends," Mom said. "You know teenaged girls."

"Didn't want to see the old man?"

"Oh, she'll see you when she gets home."

I was looking at Mom, waiting for the rest. Skating was just part of the deal she'd made with Claire. Since Uncle Albert had stayed in my bed last time, they decided he should get somebody else's bed this time, and it sure wouldn't make sense to have an old man in his nineties climb up the ladder to the top bunk, so he got Claire's room. Claire would be sleeping on a mattress in Dad's office. And I know you're wondering why Uncle Albert couldn't sleep in the office, but it's really only a big closet with a desk in it, so the camping mat had to go under the desk where your feet go. At least she wouldn't hit her head whenever she tried to sit up in the middle of the night. Also, there's no window, and I think Dad was worried that if Uncle Albert slept there, he'd never get rid of the smell.

Anyway, Claire was pretty upset about loosing her room, so they paid her off with skating and a party in January and some other stuff. I was trying to remember what I got paid off with and then it came to me. Oh yeah. Nothing. I had this nagging suspicion that Claire didn't really mind sleeping in Dad's office, but just figured it was worth some kind of trade. She's sneaky like that. I didn't mention that she'd have to fumigate her room after he left. She'd have to figure that out on her own.

Uncle Albert sat in the front seat with Dad on the way home, and I could tell that he still smelled pretty much the same. Danny was in the middle in the back, so he got it the worst. At least Mom and I had the chance to lean our faces out the window and get some fresh air.

We had pizza that night, because it was close enough to Christmas that we were out of school and Mom and Dad were off work until after the holidays, so it was kind of a celebration. Claire didn't get home until about nine o'clock, and by that time Uncle Albert was already in bed, Mom showed her that she had pulled out her pajamas and clothes for her to wear on Christmas Eve. They were folded neatly on Dad's desk. I'm not sure Claire was too happy about not being able to go and get her own clothes, but she was still pretty excited about a boy she met at the skating rink, so it didn't really matter.

Chapter 37

Quoits

The next day, we all gathered in the kitchen. Everybody had a job to do except for Dad. I guess he had a job too, since he was in charge of entertaining Uncle Albert. Danny was peeling potatoes for the mashed potatoes for Christmas dinner. I was chopping up vegetables to put in the stuffing for the turkey, and Mom and Claire were making pies for dessert. That was another part of her deal for giving up her room. She got to learn how to make apple and pumpkin pies. It looked like a whole lot more fun than chopping vegetables.

We worked for a couple of hours, and sang along with Christmas carols, until everything was ready to go into the refrigerator for Christmas dinner. Then we all got excused. Danny and I ran outside to play, and Claire went into her room to call her friends. I had a fan that Danny used in the summertime when our room got really hot, and I'd given it to her to blow out all the bad smell.

So Danny grabbed his football and we were about to head

over to the park when Dad waved to us. He and Uncle Albert were sitting at the picnic table, talking and working on something, and there were a bunch of sticks standing up the front lawn. "What's going on?" I asked.

Dad tossed me a hunk of rope. I caught it and checked it out. It looked like a piece of one of the old sisal ropes he had hanging in the garage, for tying back bushes and stuff, only he'd cut it and made it into a circle about the size of a small plate. It had been spliced, kind of like we'd learned in Boy Scouts. "What's this?" I asked.

"It's a quoit." That was Uncle Albert.

"Huh?" Now Danny was checking one out too. They were kind of interesting, but I couldn't see any possible use for them. There were four more on the table.

"Where'd you get them?" I asked.

"Made 'em." Uncle Albert said.

Ok, so they did come from the old hank of rope in the garage. I still had the football under one arm, and now put it down so that I could take a look at the braiding. Compared to what I'd learned it was pretty clean. I used both hands to try and pull it apart, just like the scout leader had done to mine. It didn't budge. Still, that begged the question. "Why? What do they do?"

"They're for Quoits," Uncle Albert said.

Sure. That made sense. After all, what was quoits without a quoit. He got up with one. I noticed then that they'd braided cloth into them so that each was a different color. Interesting. Then he walked over to one of the posts in the ground, and said, "It's a game. The goal is to throw your quoit so that it comes down over the post." He showed us how it could easily fit over the top, and then took several steps back to one of the other sticks before tossing the quoit back to the pole. It spun slowly end over end and slipped right over the top of one of the poles. Easy.

Of course, lots of things look easy until you try them yourself. I figured I'd flip my quoit over a pole, and then pick up the football and head on over to the park with Danny. I stood next to Uncle Albert, flipped my quoit like he had, and watched it land about a foot to the side of the pole.

"Now if we were actually playing," he said, "I'd score two points."

I ran over and picked up my quoit and then went back to where I'd left Uncle Albert. Danny was there now, and after he threw and missed, I took careful aim, tossed the quoit, and watched it sail over the pole, missing by about two feet. Huh. Uncle Albert flipped his again and you guessed it, right over the pole. "Four to nothing," he said.

"Wait," I said. "You obviously got to practice. I didn't." I ran over and retrieved all three quoits and then returned to the stick. Danny tossed his again. Miss. Now I could see why they were different colors. Mine was orange, and Danny's was blue. No arguing about who threw which one. I tried again. Miss. And again. I hit the pole and bounced off.

Uncle Albert had gone back to the table and was finishing the splice on another. "Let me know when you're ready," he said. "It's usually a betting game."

What? People bet on this? And why were there eight poles

hammered into the grass? I flipped another quoit and it turned lazily in the air once, twice, three times, and then slipped right over the top of the pole. "Yahoo!" I yelled and ran back to my quoit.

"Now you go on to the next pole," Uncle Albert said. Ah, now it made sense. Each pole was numbered, and you went from one to eight. Oh, and they got further and further apart too. He flipped his quoit and missed, but it came to rest leaning against the pole. He smiled and went over to pick it up. I tossed mine. It missed, but was only about three inches away. "Ah, good. Another point for me," he said. "Five to nothing."

Whoa! He got a point for missing? Then he explained. "You get two points for dropping your quoit over the top of the pole and one if nobody goes over the pole, but you're closest. Since mine was touching and yours wasn't, I got the point. It's five to nothing."

"But what about the ones where I landed right on the pole?" I asked.

Then he winked. "I wasn't playing then, so nobody got any points." Can you believe that? I just stared at him, and then he walked back over to the table. I watched him go, and could see that Dad was laughing. He was quiet about it, but he was definitely laughing at me.

I'd completely forgotten about the football by now. I said, "So you want a game?"

He looked back and I could tell that was exactly what he wanted. But he said, "It wouldn't be fair to you." Still, he walked over to the starting pole and took out his quoit. Then he took a step back, and then another step before he threw. It landed right next to the pole, but not touching it. "Now you throw," he said. I tried to move back, but he pushed me back to the spot we'd started at before. "No. Stay closer. I'll give you an advantage to even it up a bit." And he winked again.

I moved back right next to him. No old, old, old man was going to beat me and laugh about it. But he did. We played all eight poles and he won twelve to three. I got the two points when he missed the pole and I circled it, and one when my quoit ended up leaning against a pole. Other than that, he won every stake.

Claire and Mom came out then. They weren't very interested at first, but since Dad and Uncle Albert had made them their very own quoits, they had to try. And then, after just a couple of throws, it turned out that they were pretty good.

Later on, Dad went inside and brought out his old penny jar and gave everybody fifty pennies to use for betting. It didn't take very long before Claire and Uncle Albert took them all from the rest of us. Still, we left the stakes out in the lawn to practice some more on Christmas.

First Mumbley Peg and now Quoits. I guess these games were good practice back when Uncle Albert was my age. After all, he probably had to rope buffalo and go out hunting and stuff and protect himself against bears and wolves and mountain lions.

Chapter 39

Another Christmas

We didn't get up quite as early on Christmas as we used to when we were little kids, but still, we were all gathered around the tree by about nine on Christmas morning. Mom had put out a plate of blueberry muffins and fruit, and she and Dad had coffee. Uncle Albert joined us kids with hot chocolate, so it wasn't like most mornings when we raced to eat our cereal before school.

Have you ever noticed that sometimes it seems like Christmas is just an excuse for giving you clothes to the replace the ones you've outgrown? Yeah, me too. Of course, Danny never had to worry about running out of clothes, since he always got my old stuff. Anyway, once I got past the new jeans and a couple of shirts, I opened up a big, heavy box and hit the jackpot. A new skateboard, with a long deck, and upgraded wheels and bearings. I could just see myself cruising down the sidewalk on the way to middle school in the fall.

Danny was looking at it and I could tell that he was going to have to get a dishtowel just to wipe away the drool, he was so jealous. Then he started digging through his unopened packages, but it was all clothes except for one box of Hardy Boys books. Loser! I made sure that he could see how well the wheels spun on my new skateboard.

Then Dad said, "Wasn't there something else for Danny?" He helped dig around the tree for a while, and I could see by the way he was grinning, that there was definitely something there. Then he snapped his fingers. "I must have left it in the garage."

So Danny went tearing out of the living room, through the kitchen, and flew into the garage. Of course, I already knew what it was, because that was just the same thing they did with me when I was in third grade. Still, it was fun to hear him scream, "A new bike!"

Claire's big gift was a music dock for her cell phone so that she could listen to music in her room. Mom made a point of saying that if she could hear the music all the way in the kitchen, it was too loud. Still, Claire was pretty excited. She immediately got her phone and plugged the thing in right there in the living room, and then since it was Christmas, she set it to play Christmas songs.

Uncle Albert got a white shirt, but I kind of expected that, seeing as how his only shirts were stained again.

Mom got a new ring and gave Dad a big smooch right there in the living room. It was okay, I guess, but still I thought it was a little gross for old people to be acting like that.

And then Uncle Albert brought out his suitcase. "First, I have some gifts from Beattie." Uh oh. The sweaters. I'd hidden the other one down at the bottom of my underwear drawer, hoping moths would eat it, but it was still there.

He took out three boxes. Sweater boxes. I cringed. Claire looked horrified. Even Danny was old enough now to understand what had happened before. But he was the youngest, so he got to go first.

He pulled off the ribbon, and then peeled up the paper slowly and carefully, kind of like if he didn't make a mess of it, he could send it back. Finally, he took the lid off the box. Yep. A sweater. I suppose you could say it was better than the last ones that were green and yellow. This one was made up of all different color yarn, and Danny's had a good collection of blue and green and silver, and for some reason, lots of pink and yellow.

"Put it on," Mom said, "I'll take a picture for Aunt Beattie."

Danny looked at her like he'd just swallowed a tadpole, but he knew it was no use. Then he looked at his hot chocolate, and we could all tell that he was thinking of dipping it in there first, so he wouldn't have to wear it, but Mom shot out of her chair and said, "Here, I'll help you."

It was way too big, and he looked like an overgrown snow cone with a head sticking out of the top. Mom looked confused, and Danny said, "It doesn't fit. We'll have to send it back. Then Claire said, "I'll bet it's Billy's. Open yours and take a look."

Sure enough. The one in my box was too small. "She must have mixed them up," Mom said with a smile, and traded mine with Danny's.

I tried to give Claire my nastiest look, but she just laughed, so I said, "Go ahead princess. I'll bet yours is the best of all."

That got her, and she looked really nervous. She opened one corner of the box and peeked inside, and then smiled. Huh? She was smiling? Must be just to try and fool us, but when she opened the box, there was a blue sweater, a style I'd seen her wear before, and in her favorite color. What happened?

"Oh, there's a note," she said. She opened the envelope and took out a card and started to read.

Dear Claire,

I'm sorry but I ran out of the pretty colorful yarn and the store was all out of everything except for this blue. I hope you're not too disappointed. I'll get right to work on another sweater as soon as they get their new yarn order.

Aunt Beattie

What? Claire pulled the sweater over her head without anyone telling her to, and even I had to admit that it would have looked really good on her even if she hadn't been grinning ear to ear. Sometimes life just isn't fair. And then I remembered the last line of the letter. Aunt Beattie was going to make another for her. Ah. Delayed gratification. I could live with that.

After all the pictures, and Mom took a lot so that she could embarrass us from every possible angle, Uncle Albert said, "And I brought some presents for the kids too."

Chapter 39

Uncle Albert Strikes Again

Hmm. Interesting. More marbles with weird disappearing letters on them? More strange stories about smoke ladies in the forest? I'd really been looking forward to something like that, but at the same time, I was a little nervous. After all, last time he gave me the gift of presence, and I ended up having to be principal. I wondered what this one would be.

They were in boxes, three of them. I took mine and looked at it. It was just a little rectangle, about an inch, by an inch, by about six inches long. Danny's and Claire's were the same. I tried not to look too nervous while I opened it.

I tore off the paper and found a wooden box. Inside was a pocketknife that fit perfectly in the wooden box. Wow! I just had to open it up right away. It had two nice sharp blades, one that opened up at either end. I showed it to Dad, and he smiled and nodded. "You should probably close the blades before you cut somebody." But I could tell he was impressed. It was way bigger than the knife I'd gotten when I was a little kid, and looked much better made.

By now, both Danny and Claire had opened their boxes. While my knife had a bone handle, Danny's was smaller with a red plastic cover. Claire's was the same size as mine, but it was pink ivory. She opened it up one blade at a time. Yep, just the same. Then I started thinking. Hadn't I seen something like that before?

Mom asked to see Claire's knife and then got up. In a few seconds, she was back from the kitchen with the pocketknife she kept in the gadget drawer. "It's just like mine," she said. She looked up at Uncle Albert. "Was this from you?"

He nodded. "I dropped by your house one Christmas back when you was about six." She looked confused and he said, "You probably don't remember. I couldn't stay long, just a few hours." He took the knife from her. "Yeah. I remember this one. One of my best. I think your folks put it away. They wanted to hold it until you got a little older." He flipped it over, opened the larger blade, and held it up close to his face, like he was looking for something. And then he smiled.

"They told me it was from my uncle, but I always figured they meant Uncle Jack. I don't remember even hearing about you until Beattie wrote."

"Probably not," he laughed. "I was traveling quite a bit back when you was a girl."

I was thinking about what Uncle Albert had said. I didn't think anyone else caught it. Maybe it was because I'd gotten pretty good at trying to hear the details when I was filling in for Mr. Johnson as principal and I had a couple of kids sent to me for fighting. I looked over at him. "What did you mean, one of your best?"

"Used to make pocket knives. That was how I made my living. Still do sometimes." He reached out like he wanted mine, and I handed it to him. He flipped it over, kind of like how he'd done Mom's, and opened up the larger blade. "Right there," he said. I bent over to look. I'd noticed something before, but figured it was just a smudge. Now that I looked really carefully, I could see tiny writing engraved in it. 'A. Saloozian.' Cool. I had a knife engraved by a master knife maker, and he was my very own great, great, great uncle.

We all checked out each of the knives, and then Uncle Albert looked at my mom and dad and said, "Sorry I didn't bring anything for you folks, but I figure Christmas is mostly for the kids."

"No problem," Dad said. "These are beautifully made. How did you learn to make pocket knives?"

Well, that launched Uncle Albert into a long story about an old man who'd been living out in the forest back when he was about sixteen. Remember the forest by his house, where he met the smoke lady and got his pouch full of marbles? I guess he'd been hiking one day when it started to storm. He was several miles from home, so he decided that the best thing to do was to build a little shelter and hunker down for the night. He had some water and a sandwich in his backpack for food, so he figured he was okay and just needed a fire for warmth and to keep any wild animals away.

Well, he talked and talked for almost an hour and when he was all done, we'd heard about the old man who saw his smoke and came out and rescued him when the rain put out the fire and collapsed his shelter, and how the storm lasted for nine days and all that time he had to sleep on the floor of the cottage out in the forest. That story was full of mystery and magic, and Old Boot, the man's dog, who knew Uncle Albert was out in the storm even before it started to rain. I guess the man taught him all kinds of useful things, like making knives, and building furniture, and even how to do magic tricks and play the flute. But I think I'll have to save that story for another day. It's a little too long for now.

When we were cleaning up, I found another marble. It was buried down in the bottom of my sweater box, and with all the wrapping paper, I hadn't even seen it. It had a 'P' on it, and I wondered if it was the same one I'd gotten in fourth grade, so I ran into my room and checked my desk drawer. Nope. The old one was still there.

So I came back out to the living room. Uncle Albert was there, looking at me. Before I could say a word, he said, "Perseverance."

"Huh," I said.

"Your marble. I see you found it." Then he looked at my brother and sister. "Go ahead. Take a look in your sweater boxes. I chose this time. You each have one."

Okay. I could understand if one of us didn't find the marble in the sweater box, but all three? How was that even possible? I started to think about what he'd been doing while we opened the sweater boxes and later when we opened the knives. He was just sitting there in Dad's chair. He never moved, and I didn't see him toss the marbles into the boxes. But they couldn't have been there all along. At least one of us would have seen a black marble, or heard it rattling. It must have been the smoke lady.

"So what's persa... mean?" I couldn't remember the word.

"Perseverance. It means if you get a job, you'll stick to it and do it right, like when you were principal last fall."

I shot a look at Mom and Dad, and they just shook her heads. "You didn't tell him?" Then I turned to the others. "Danny? Claire? Who told?" They both shrugged too, and I could tell they really hadn't said anything. This was getting spooky.

He was looking at Claire. She'd found her marble now. "It's a 'W,'" she said.

"What do you think?" he asked. When she shrugged her shoulders, he said, "Wisdom."

She looked pretty confused, so he said, "You are very wise for your age. In fact, telling Billy about how everyone wanted to dump the monkey on their back on him when he was principal was a perfect example."

Mom looked at her. "What monkey?" she said.

Ok. So he didn't hear from Mom, and Dad was laughing. "I like that. Dumping a monkey. I'd never heard of that."

But it was clear that nobody had told Uncle Albert about that either, and I never told anybody, and from the look on Claire's face, she never did either. Did I mention this was getting spooky?

Danny's marble had an 'L' on it for Listener. And I

thought back to all of our walks home from school when I was principal, and how I talked and talked and talked and talked some more, and Danny just listened, and asked a question once in a while. It was like he was there just to give me a chance to try to think aloud and work out all of my challenges every day. In fact, now that I think about it, he may have been the one who suggested a homework club after I told him about all of the parents who were frustrated that their kids didn't have any place to do homework at home. Hmm. Listener.

Epilogue

Well, I guess that's my story. Now you can look at the back of the book. Remember, where you were supposed to write down your three guesses about what you thought my problem was? You did do that, didn't you? How many guessed, 'Mr. Johnson will run away from the school and you'll have to take over as principal?' Or even just, 'You'll be a principal?' Yeah, sure. I know lots of you are going to say that you knew all along, but you can't fool me. You guessed something else and now you're just trying to make it up to make yourselves look smart, but remember, I'm a kid too, and I've tried that trick, so put down your pencils and don't try writing any new stuff in the back of the book.

Where do you think I got that idea? I always write down my three guesses about what kind of problem a kid's going to have in a book just inside the back cover, and I read lots of books, and I never guess right. Well sometimes I do, but I figure it doesn't count if I sneak a peek in the middle of the book just to see what's going on. Hey, maybe that's why you got it right too!

There are a couple of other things Mr. Ward said I needed to write. So here's number one. You can't play Mumblety Peg unless you get your parent's permission. It can be dangerous. And you can only play it with a pocketknife, not your mom's good kitchen knives. Here's another. Before you cut up your dad's rope out in the garage to make quoits, you'd better check with him. Otherwise, you might get in lots of trouble, and now that I told you, you won't be able to blame it on me. Here's the last one. Mr. Ward says there's no such thing as a smoke lady in the forest and no boy is going to go for a hike and end up spending nine days in some old cabin in the forest with a man who makes knives and a dog named Old Boot who knows who's out there even before they get there. And he also says that nobody can make letters appear and disappear on marbles. I have to write that because he's giving me a grade, and he told me to, but I know better, because I know Uncle Albert. And now, so do you.

ABOUT THE AUTHOR

Just a little about me. I am a retired businessman, teacher, and school principal. Most of the stories in this book relate directly to my experience in and around schools. You might wonder if Billy was exaggerating when he said that he was to blame that the kids went home with dirty clothes after the food fight. Of course, the principal gets blamed for everything, from dirty clothes, to lost sweaters, to poor grades. It's part of the job. Also, I knew both the thumper and the growler, as well as lots of outstanding teachers like Mr. Ward and Ms. Gonzales. I valued parents who supported their kids, but also held them accountable for their behavior. Unfortunately, I also knew a few whose kids could do no wrong. Who do you suppose did better in school?

I actually wrote <u>Uncle Albert</u> while camping in the Big Trees State Park in California. We'd hike in the morning, and then relax in the afternoon, and that gave me the chance to write. It was a fun write, and I found myself laughing out loud about Billy's problems while I worked. I hope you find some laughs here too.

I'm the father of one daughter and the grandfather of two delightful little kids. I hope that someday, one of them has the chance to be principal, if only for a day.

OTHER BOOKS BY STEPHEN GILBERT

The Santa Hat is a shorter story about a third grade boy who moves with his mother to a new community. It tells of his experiences making new friends, and the man he comes to consider his father. It's written at about a second to third grade reading level.

The Ruby Ring is a two part series that includes, The Ruby Ring, Casting The Die, and Seizing The Crown. They tell the story of a Robert, a teen aged boy, his twin sister Marie, and their best friend, Johnny. It's set in an imaginary medieval kingdom, ruled by an evil duke. Robert and Marie's father is killed early in the story, and his mother gives Robert a large ruby ring that glows brightly whenever he puts it on. As he learns later, it is the traditional ring of kingship, and now it's his. The story tells of the battle between Robert, Duke Henry, and their followers to possess the ring, and ultimately, the kingdom. The stories include adventure, swordplay, and magic. The third book in the series should be out soon. These books are written at about a fifth to sixth grade reading level.

I've included the first chapters of The Ruby Ring below.

PROLOGUE

The woman digging in the garden was neither young nor old. Her hair, tied back in a simple green bandana, had that salt and pepper quality that might come at any age. Her drab brown dress was long and flowing, and any observer would be able to tell from looking at her hands that she was accustomed to hard work.

She paused in her digging to wipe a stream of sweat from her brow, leaving a brown smear that traveled across her forehead. The night was hot, just as she remembered it being eighteen years earlier. She shuddered suddenly, squeezing her eyes tightly together. One lonely tear broke free, staining a path through the dirt on her cheek and giving voice to her sadness. There was much to do though, and grieving would have to wait until later. She paused to compose herself with a drink of water from a chipped clay jug, and then resumed her digging.

When she judged that the hole was deep enough, she let go her spade and dropped to her knees. Working swiftly now, she used her hands to cast out small piles of soil. Presently, she hit a hard surface and grimaced. She'd remembered. The object that she had been seeking was to one side of the hole, so she used the spade to enlarge the space, and then bent down and using her fingers, carefully scooped away the remaining dirt. She looked carefully about her before reaching into the hole with both hands, and prizing out a small box, approximately the size of an apple. The rotting cloth in which it had been wrapped tore as she pulled the box from the hole, so she slowed and carefully wound it again to hide the wooden container.

Laying the package to one side, she took up the spade again and quickly filled in the hole, taking the time to sweep dry dirt and leaves over the opening so that it might appear to the casual observer to have been undisturbed. With a satisfied nod, she picked up her treasure and made her way back to the house, stepping carefully around the beans, squash, and tomatoes.

PART ONE
ROBERT OF MASDEN

CHAPTER 1
MASDEN

Robert breathed deeply and grounded the heavy wooden practice sword. His father, sweat rolling off his muscular chest, drove his own sword into the dirt and panted, "Enough?"

Robert's shallow laugh betrayed his eagerness to train, "Never. But it looked like you could use some water." He went to the basin in the corner of the stable and dipped a tin cup, bringing up some of the clear, cold water.

His father looked at him, his lips forming a comical grin, "I could use some water! Why you young pup! Sixteen and brash as can be!" He chuckled and said, "Well, I suppose a drink would taste good." Pointing his finger at his son, he chuckled, "You were about to get whipped and you know it!" Still, he took the offered cup and drained it in a single gulp. He scooped another cupful and splashed it across his upper torso. "You're getting better. I do believe that one day soon, you'll pass me up." He patted his son's shoulder and added, "but not today, and not tomorrow!" Then he laughed, "enough play. We've both got work to do. Have you finished the repairs to the miller's saddle?"

Robert shook his head. "Not yet. A few hours work, and I'll be done." He pointed to the horse in one of the stable's larger stalls. "He does have a fine horse, doesn't he?"

His father laughed. "He does indeed, much too fine for stable masters like us." He hung the cup on the hook by the basin and turned serious. "You get your chores done. I want some help with the books later this afternoon. It's time you learn how the business is run."

§§§§

Later that evening, father and son walked slowly through the village, their day's work done. Already, candles were starting to flicker in the windows, a testament to long hours spent at the stable. Several times, Robert started to open his mouth, but then held his tongue, and walked on. Finally, as they rounded a corner and saw the welcoming glow coming from the windows of their own small cottage at the end of the lane, he decided to speak.

"Father, I don't understand."

His father turned to him and wiped away a shock of tawny hair just starting to give way to gray. "What don't you understand son?"

Robert paused, as if trying to find the proper words. His father was a big man, a man of authority. Though he sought no position of leadership in the village, others naturally listened when he spoke, and several sought his counsel. Robert had always been awed by the man's strength and bearing and had noticed that even his friends treated his father with a deference that they seldom showed to others. He paused and then plunged ahead. "Why do you work me so hard? Johnny and the others went fishing today, but I've been working. Last week while I practiced ciphers after work, they were down at the river swimming. It doesn't seem fair."

His father nodded slowly and grunted. "It doesn't, does it? So you think you'd prefer to be down at the river?"

Gaining his courage, Robert blurted, "Yes." He was about to add more when his father waved him to an old log lying under a grove of pine trees near the house.

"Have a seat. Maybe it's time that we talk."

Robert went to the log and then watched as his father eased himself carefully down with a sigh. He'd noticed him limping slightly on the walk home and wondered if the old jagged scar that wrapped across the front of his left leg was bothering him. He'd asked about it once when he was a young boy and been told only that it was from an old injury, and not to worry. "Is your leg bothering you today?"

His father waved his hand as if to silence him. "I probably just tweaked it a bit during the sword practice. It'll go away." Then he smiled. "Do I work you too hard?" Robert nodded and thinking that this was his opening, started to speak but his father interrupted him. "You're no longer a boy, Robert. You're becoming a man." He looked at his son. "And that means that you have to be willing to take on the responsibilities of a man. And a man…"

Robert interrupted him. "I understand all that father, but the others. They do their chores and then they have freedom to do other things. I study at school and do my chores, and then I must practice reading and writing and figures. And lately I have to read and write in the old tongue. It seems a waste of time!"

"Are you done?" asked the older man with a wry grin.

Robert started to speak and then shrugged his shoulders. "I think I've said my piece."

His father looked at him and smiled. To look into his son's face was like peering into a looking glass that erased the age from his own. "How many of your friends can read?"

Robert started. "Well Johnny can read pretty well, and some of the others can read some, at least from the simpler books."

"And you?"

"I think I read well, Father. At least, I don't know of any books that I can't read."

"Neither do I. Why do you suppose that's the case?"

Robert smiled ruefully. "I suppose it's the work." Then he added quickly, "but what's the need? If I'm to be a stable master like you, what will I need to read?" Sensing a strong argument, he added, "And I certainly won't need to read and write in the old tongue!" He looked up at his father's face triumphantly but what he heard next shattered his victory.

"And why would you be a stable master?"

Robert didn't know what to say. He sputtered, "I...but...doesn't every boy take over his father's trade?"

"Is that what you want?" his father asked seriously, "to spend your life covered in manure and tending to the needs of travelers? To care for fine horses while riding nothing better than a nag yourself?"

As he stared at his father, Robert was struck speechless. "I...what else could I do?"

The older man smiled and stretched out his leg. "Ah, now we get to the heart of the matter. Always remember this. Set your goals high, and let your effort define your character."

Robert frowned. It was a phrase he'd heard often from his father. He was about to speak when his father looked up at the glow from the cottage window. "Go up to the house and tell your mother that we're home and that we'll be in for dinner shortly." Robert rose and he added, "and bring us each a flask of ale. This talking is thirsty work."

When Robert returned, he could see that his father was standing, flexing and stretching out his injured leg. He watched for a moment until his father noticed him and waved him over. When he handed him the flask, the man took a long draft and then sighed and wiped his mouth with the back of his sleeve.

"Ah, that was good. I thank you." He motioned Robert back to his seat on the log and settled himself. "So you want to know why you must learn to read and write in both the common verse and in the tongue of the ancients." He looked across at his son.

Robert nodded.

"You said yourself that most of your friends struggle to read at all, and yet you read fluently. Am I right?" Without waiting, he continued. "You have great ability Robert." He tapped the side of his head with one finger. "A fine mind and a curiosity that places you above the others. Your mother and I have known that since you were a babe. Your sister shares these traits, for all that she is a girl, and that is why I teach you together."

Robert nodded. It was most uncommon for anyone to bother to teach girls in the village, and yet his sister if anything, could read and write better than he, though she had little interest in numbers.

"It is said," his father continued, "that to those who receive great gifts from the gods shall come great responsibilities." He took a large mouthful of beer and swirled it around before swallowing with a sigh. "The gods have a plan for you Robert, and I would be remiss in my responsibilities were I to fail to prepare you."

Robert's head swirled with this new information. The thought of not following his father into the stable was more than a little bit frightening, but somehow he knew that the man was right. He would not be happy as a stable master. His friends, while fine companions, often teased his learning and seemed uncomfortable with him when he referred to something that he had read. He looked at his father, "But what am I to become?"

The man smiled. "Ah, so I have your interest." He rose and flung the remnants of his beer onto the grass. "Don't forget that we live in uncertain times, and you must be prepared for whatever may come your way. That is why you must work hard to master both the new and the old tongues. It is also why a stable master's son trains with the wooden sword." He patted Robert on the shoulder. "I fear though, that that is a much longer conversation than we have time for tonight." He paused and then smiled indulgently at his son. "Tomorrow's Saturday. I'll work the stable alone, and you can take the day to relax with your friends. Come. I smell dinner."

CHAPTER 2
JOHNNY TUPPENCE

Robert looked enviously at the tall young man walking next to him. "What bait were you using? I didn't get so much as a nibble, and you've got what, eight fine trout?"

Laughing, Johnny Tuppence said, "Ah, the secrets of the trade my boy. We dug the worms together this morning. Did you forget? It was my superior skill."

"Bah," continued Robert. He looked at his partner's tackle. They had similar equipment, rough hewn fishing poles whittled from willow branches along with fine woolen thread and hooks fashioned from metal fragments scrounged at the blacksmith's yard. "Johnny...You are planning to share, right?"

His friend draped an arm around his shoulder. "Of course," he replied seriously. "I managed to hook a little sunfish earlier. It's all bones and fins, but you're welcome to it!" Seeing Robert's scowl, he burst into laughter. "I'll tell you what. I need four fish for dinner tonight. The rest are yours. I'll throw in the sunfish as a bonus."

The two friends continued up the lightly forested trail, chattering about their fishing trip, and soon made their way over a small rise. From the top, they could see the village of Masden laid out before them. It was a small community of some thirty homes, surrounded by a patchwork quilt of vegetable gardens and fields of grains.

The center of the village was dominated by church and inn, standing across from one another, one representing the spiritual and the other the temporal heart of the community.

As they started down the slope, Johnny squinted and said, "Do you see the cloud of dirt in the distance there?"

Robert laughed. "Your eyes are better than mine. I see something. What do you suppose it is? Horsemen?"

Shading his eyes with his hand and taking a long look, Johnny answered, "I'd guess so. They're probably a couple of hours away." Then he looked at Robert, "Say, let's stop by the tavern. My uncle's just cracked a new keg of beer."

His friend glanced at him and shook his head. "I've no money for beer. Besides, I need to get these fish home to my mother."

"It's on me," Johnny insisted. "Just one and then I'll send you on your way."

"On you?" replied Robert. "I've never known you to pay for beer. On your uncle you mean?"

Johnny laughed. "Not at all. I figure I'll give him my share of the trout, so he'll be more than happy to draw us a couple of mugs."

Laughing, Robert pounded him on the shoulder. "Always the schemer. That must be why I stick around you."

§§§§

Two hours later, Robert sat down with the family for dinner. His father led them in a quick prayer, and then everyone dug into the fresh trout. After taking a bite and savoring the buttery flavor, he turned to his son, "It would appear that your luck was good. Where'd you go fishing today?"

Robert looked at him. "You know the old willow on the far bank of the creek? Just beyond it's an inlet where the moss overhangs the water. The fish like to rest there."

His father chuckled, "I know it well. And Johnny? How'd he do?"

Robert grimaced, "Actually, these are his." He shook his head. "He says he talks to them, warns them about my hook and tells them to come to him." Then he laughed and took another bite of his fish. "Can you imagine? Talking to fish?"

His father smiled and said softly, "His father used to say the same thing to me."

Robert looked surprised, "Really? I just thought it was something Johnny was putting on. Good fish though." He took a bite and looked up at his father, "Oh, by the way, where were the riders from?"

His father looked at him. "Riders?"

"Yes. Johnny and I saw them coming down the east-west road. We figured they'd put their horses up in the stable before they went on to the inn."

"I saw no riders. How far out were they?"

"We could just see the dust on the horizon from the hilltop. A couple of hours I'd suppose. Maybe they're still on the road."

His father stirred the fish around on his plate, as he snuck a nervous glance at his wife. "Maybe." Then he smiled. "After dinner I'll go check with the innkeeper. I'm sure they'll want a place for their mounts." Forcing a smile back onto his face, he looked around the table, his eyes lighting on his daughter. While Robert took after his father, his twin shared her mother's dark hair and brown eyes. Though her features were soft and delicate, there was an underlying strength that seemed to radiate out from her. "And you, Marie, how was your day?"

"Busy," she said with a smile. "Sally was here. We worked on a new cable stitch on the sweaters we're knitting and after that, we read from the book of poetry."

Robert groaned. "It's Saturday. Take a break from schoolwork!"

His father turned to him, "Don't forget our talk. You'd be wise to work on your own lessons a little more."

He was about to say more when Marie interrupted him, "Robert does well in school, father. He's the top scholar in the class in all subjects, without really seeming to try and he's far more fluent than I am in the old tongue that you've been teaching us." She grinned at her brother. "Besides, had he been working with me on computations, we'd be eating potatoes instead of this trout."

"That's right Father. I..."

His father interrupted him. "Well mister hard worker. I trust you're well rested after spending the afternoon under that willow tree. How about if you finish your dinner? I'll need your help at the stables when those riders come in."

Robert nodded curtly, "Yes sir."

§§§§

The riders didn't show up that night. Robert spent two hours mucking out the stalls and laying new straw for the horses they boarded before returning to his work on the miller's saddle. His father had passed the time pulling out the old worn tack, and setting it aside for repair the following week. He was replacing the leather in one of the harnesses when Robert came up to him. "It's getting dark, Father. I imagine they've passed us by."

His father nodded and continued working the tough leather straps. "Possibly. Doesn't seem likely though. They'd have had to go through town. Maybe we'll see them tomorrow. They could have camped on the road." He finished tying a knot and stretched the harness out on a worktable. "Well, this will wait until tomorrow. Let's head for home."

Once out in the street, he looked across to the inn. They could hear the raised voices of the Saturday night revelers. "I hear you and Johnny tasted William's new porter. How was it?"

Robert smiled. "Good. Better than the last batch, I think. A little bitter, but it went down well on a hot day. Shall we go in?"

"I think not son." He continued walking down the dusty road. "You're mother and sister will worry if we're late." He looked up the road to their home. The warm glow of a candle flickered in the front window. Throwing his arm around his son's shoulder, he said, "Those were fine trout you brought today. I wish we could eat like that every Saturday night." He grew quiet as they walked along, finally saying. "I was thinking of riding up to the old hill fort tomorrow after church. Why don't you bring Johnny along?"

Robert was puzzled. The hill fort had been abandoned generations ago. So far as he knew, it was empty and run down, an isolated place. He looked at his father. "Sure. What do you want to do?"

His father punched him playfully in the shoulder. "You'll see."

CHAPTER 3
ATTACKED!

Robert woke to the sound of pounding on the front door. Bleary eyed, he looked out the window in the loft and saw that it was still dark outside. He heard rustling downstairs and then his father's voice calling, "Who's there?"

In response, the door slammed open with a splintering crash. Robert jumped from his bed and sprinted to look out over the rail to the main room downstairs. A heavily armed man stepped into the living room. He could see two others directly behind him. His mind flashed on the dust cloud on the road earlier that afternoon. Could these be the riders? Why were they here? Before he could react, he heard his father roar, "Get out of my house!"

The man turned toward the voice in the bedroom that his parents shared and motioned to the others. He pulled a short sword out of a scabbard at his waist and raised it as he stepped cautiously forward. Just then, Robert saw the flash of a blade come from beneath him, and the sword went clattering to the floor. With a howl of pain, the man pulled back the bloody stump that remained of his arm.

Wide eyed, Robert saw his father emerge from the bedroom, wearing his bedclothes and carrying a heavy two-handed broadsword. The other two men were in the room now, each armed with a short fighting blade. They circled Robert's father warily, looking for advantage. As each man lunged forward, his father parried their thrusts, leaving them frustrated. Slowly the taller of the two men worked his way around to the side of the room. Like mad dogs, they continued to thrust and parry until they had forced him back into the corner.

Robert raced down the stairs and grabbed the poker from the fireplace. He lifted it over his head and was about to advance when his father shouted, "Get out of here. Take your mother and sister and run to the place we were going to tomorrow. I'll meet you there."

"Father," he yelled and stepped forward with the poker.

"Go," he shouted, but Robert wasn't listening. With a thud, he brought the poker down on the shorter man's right shoulder, stunning his arm and forcing him to drop his weapon. The man turned, and pulling a dagger from his belt with his left hand, jumped at Robert.

Robert leaped back and struck out with the poker, barely missing the man's weapon.

The other man looked aside in confusion, and then pressed his fight home against Robert's father. He lunged, and then skittered to one side as Robert's father parried with his long sword. Back and forth they raged, the invader attacking and Robert's father skillfully parrying his jabs.

Warily, Robert and the shorter man circled one another, each looking for an opening. As Robert stepped back into the doorway to his parent's bedroom, he caught sight of his mother, arms wrapped around Marie, holding her head to her breast. "Run Mother," he yelled. "Out the window!" Just then the man slashed with his dagger and Robert thrust his hips back as the blade cut the front of his nightshirt. As the man was recovering, he slashed at him with the poker and was rewarded with a crunch of bone as the heavy end bit into his cheek. He folded onto the floor and Robert yelled again, "Run now!" He looked back in time to see his mother pushing Marie out the window, and then returned his gaze to the fight. The man he'd struck was rising to his knees, his face a mass of blood. Robert swung down hard, slamming the poker through the top of the man's skull and dropping him to the floor.

He looked back into the corner to see that the taller of the robbers had taken advantage of his greater maneuverability with his short blade to push his way inside the reach of the long sword, and was grappling with his father. Robert reached down and grabbed the dead man's sword and leapt into the fight just in time to see his father's bad leg buckle. As he reached out to save his balance, the man plunged a dagger into his chest.

"No!" he yelled and jumped forward with the sword. His opponent turned lightly on his feet, letting Robert's father slump to the floor, grappling weakly with the blade that protruded from his body.

As Robert charged him, the tall man slashed his blade to the side and then grazed him on the head with the hilt of the weapon. Dazed, Robert dropped to his knees and rolled into the wall. The man smiled wickedly and walked to where Robert huddled. As he raised the weapon to finish him off, Robert plunged his sword up and into the man's stomach. The man's eyes went wide and he looked down at the bloody stain that had appeared on his robe. Then he slumped backward and fell slowly to the floor.

Robert rose carefully and looked around at the carnage. Two of the invaders were lying on the floor, their eyes rolled upward in the posture of the dead. The third lay whimpering in a pool of blood in one corner, trying weakly to staunch the bleeding of his stump.

He turned to his father, still pulling weakly at the knife that protruded from his chest. Kneeling tenderly by his side, he brushed his hand across his forehead. "You'll be OK. I'll get the doctor."

His father shook his head wearily. "It's too late. You must listen to me now. Take your mother and your sister and go to the hill fort. I've left a cache of food and supplies in a cavern under the old temple. You'll be safe there for a few days."

"But…"

His father's response was savage. "No time. You've got to get out of here. They'll be back. Go quickly; take your mother and flee!"

"But they're dead father, we've killed them."

His father shook his head and whispered, "There will be more. Look at their uniforms, their weapons. These are the Duke's men. When these men don't report in, he'll send more." He dropped his chin to his chest and took a few haggard breaths. Raising his head slightly he said, "Remind your mother to take the coins I've hidden in the attic and the old box she buried in the garden." He lifted his head slowly and looked weakly into Robert's eyes. "You've been all I could have hoped for in a son. Go now and make me proud. Be gone before sunrise." With a last rattling breath, he dropped his head and slid to the floor.

Robert sat still, stroking his father's forehead as the tears streamed down his cheeks. He was roused out of his lethargy by a scream from outside.

Leaping up, he grabbed a sword and ran to the door in time to see a horseman flying down the road, his mother screaming in pursuit. She stopped and slumped to her knees, wringing her hands in despair. Robert raced to her side and lifted her to her feet. "There was another man outside," she wailed. "He's got Marie!"

Made in the USA
San Bernardino, CA
23 March 2017